USA *Today* Bestselling Author

Dale Mayer

TERK'S GUARDIANS
LANGDON 04

LANGDON: TERK'S GUARDIANS, BOOK 4
Beverly Dale Mayer
Valley Publishing Ltd.

ISBN-13: 978-1-778862-93-9
Print Edition

Books in This Series:

About This Book

Langdon hasn't been in a good place for a long time, but it was time enough to chase away the woman he'd loved since forever. Unable to reach her to make it right, he realizes she's disappeared—and not by choice. He then finds out why Molly was kidnapped and by whom.

Molly would do just about anything for Langdon, yet being used as leverage to force him to act wasn't part of the plan. But escaping would take more than her special energy skills, abilities her captors are unaware of. She needs to keep it that way.

Now if only she could open the psychic door she'd slammed shut between her and Langdon to let him know what was happening—before he was forced to do something that could kill them both …

Sign up to be notified of all Dale's releases here!
https://geni.us/DaleNews

PROLOGUE

BOJAN SMILED AT the group and announced, "We'll probably be back and forth. I really have no idea how this will work."

Bullard shrugged. "As you've already seen, we have lots of people going back and forth with some regularity, so it's really fine with us. Any time you want to come, it's all good, and we'll be happy to have you."

Lacy walked over to where Leia held the twins, now six weeks old. Lacy kissed all three of them. "You look after these two, *huh*? Just remember to put them down once in a while," she teased, with a grin. "It's good for all of you."

"Oh, stop. I'm not that bad." Leia looked up at her friend, with a huge smile. "You have no idea how grateful I am."

"Your face tells me every day," Lacy declared, as she crouched in front of them. "We'll be back, and, in a couple years, we'll come again to repeat the process."

At that future mention, his shock clearly evident on his facial expression, Bullard stammered, "Wait, what?"

Leia looked at Lacy in delight. "Seriously?"

Lacy nodded, then leaned forward and whispered, "Girls next time." She stepped back and winked at Leia, then gave Bullard a big hug. "We're off to Terkel's place because chaos is about to begin over there."

"It's bound to happen," Bullard noted, "but no babies yet, right?"

"Not yet, but it won't be long, and I'm hoping to get some training in. Although Terkel says I should be training some people over there, but that's hardly the case."

Bullard nodded. "Whatever Terkel's got planned, you go for it. We're just glad to have you as part of the family."

And, with Bojan and Lacy holding hands, the two of them said goodbye to the rest of the group.

As they headed to the airport, where Bullard's plane was waiting to take them to England, Lacy looked up at Bojan. "Kind of amazing that we have this much family all over the place."

"I know," Bojan agreed. "Are you okay to go to Terkel's place?"

"We need to," she said, "and it's probably really where we belong, but we should definitely come back and forth."

"Absolutely."

They boarded the plane and waited for the pilot to say they were ready to take off.

Bojan's phone rang. "Hello, Terkel. … Yeah, we're on the plane right now, just waiting to take off. … Okay. Sure, that's not a problem. The more the merrier, as they say. Who is it?"

Just then, somebody bolted onto the plane, then looked up at Bojan and smiled.

Bojan laughed and told Terk, "It's all good. He's here."

She looked over at Riff. "I saw you at the dividing wall, when the shooting was going on."

He laughed. "Yeah, you sure did. Two of those shots were mine, taking out the gunman," he shared. "I tend to be there, but not there, … kind of turning up in odd places, wherever I'm needed."

She frowned at him. "Does Bullard know?"

"He does, but now I'm heading back because Terkel apparently has another case."

"I hope it doesn't involve me," Bojan added. "I need a little downtime."

"Oh, that's all right. He's hoping to use you for security at home," Riff shared. "It's for someone else."

At that, Terkel's voice came through loud and clear to all three of them. *Bojan, it's about an old friend of yours. Langdon Morrissey is his name.*

Yeah, I know him, but why?

He reached out after hearing from a woman who could be in trouble. I think he tried to reach you as well but you were out of commission.

Right, so what does he want?

Something about his mother being murdered and her caregiver being kidnapped.

At that, Bojan frowned. *Seriously?*

Yeah.

Langdon is awesome, but she's not his mother.

Terkel replied, *I got that.*

She's one of the cabinet ministers, Bojan added. *He talks about her as being his mother, but it's not in a biological sense. He was one of those extra kids who came home one day and stayed. But the caregiver, now that's interesting. I thought her caregiver was Molly.*

That's the name I have. Apparently Molly's been kidnapped.

Ah, hell. This shit just never ends.

I'm sending Rick over as backup. Langdon already has some leads, but he doesn't want to go into this blind, and he under-

stands that we have some skills, Terk shared, with a laugh.

Yeah, that's because he has skills himself, Bojan noted. *So, if he's looking for backup, he's expecting it to get ugly. I can go*, he offered, looking over at Lacy.

No, if we need you, we'll call you, Terkel replied, sounding adamant. *Bullard is also sending over Eton, who will be there to help out. However, if this Langdon guy's got skills, I'd like to know what kind of skills we're talking about.*

Yeah, you and me both. He's never really talked to me about it. I just know they exist.

Seems to be the right time to find out.

I'm wondering why Langdon hasn't gone after Molly, Riff noted, with a frown.

Bojan looked up at him and nodded. *Good question, and they used to be an item, by the way. But I also know that Langdon was heading in for surgery. He's missing a leg but had a couple ribs rebuilt in order to protect his lungs. That was the last I heard, but I don't know what happened after that.*

Maybe his health is stopping him from rescuing Molly then, as something is off if he asked for help.

Absolutely. He's always been a loner but a can-do type of guy. And he would never ask for help.

This time he did, Terk murmured. *And help he'll get.*

Bojan nodded. *That makes sense, because Molly was his heart.*

And he'll get all the help he needs, Terk declared.

CHAPTER 1

LANGDON MORRISSEY STARED balefully down at the toes on his remaining foot, as he stood in his London apartment. He didn't know to what extent the metal in his body was causing the disruption in his energy, but the lack of a leg was causing a major disruption on his mindset. He knew he was supposed to adapt, to just deal with it and move on, but whoever came up with that bit of wisdom obviously hadn't been in the position of having to deal with it.

Nobody who had experienced such a thing would be so cavalier as to pass it on to someone in this position. Langdon was mostly dealing with it, and, though he was still struggling to a certain extent, he was getting there. He had bigger issues than most, and, while that might make him sound like some sort of a princess, he was not. The fact of the matter was, he had nobody to talk to about this.

On the up-and-up, he had no idea how to reframe these physical losses in his head with what was happening in his life, particularly when it came to the other aspect of his special energy abilities, and that was something he was rather desperate to fix. He could talk to Terk, yet Terk didn't have the same issues. There weren't very many energy workers to begin with—and even they differed from the others with their own gifts—and Langdon didn't know of any who shared his particular problem, where the metal rods and staples in his body were messing with his energy field.

Terk would say that the issue was more mental than anything, and, if so, nobody could help Langdon with that issue. Although that wasn't being fair to Terk, because Langdon hadn't told Terk what the issue was. Right now Langdon had additional bigger problems. His phone buzzed just then, and he snatched it up off the table. "Well?"

Terk was on the other end. Of course he was.

In a mild voice, as if Terk knew exactly what was going on in Langdon's head but was choosing to ignore it, Terk replied, "Rick is on his way to you right now. His ETA is less than two hours."

Langdon closed his eyes in relief, as he muttered a guttural thank-you.

Terk added, "Anytime you want help with the other issues, you know you only have to ask."

Langdon winced at that. "Yeah, but you don't even know what I'm going through," he snapped, his tone unfortunately harsh.

After a moment of silence, Terk let out a note of laughter. "None of us will know if you don't at least try to explain," Terk noted. "You might be surprised at how much some of us do know and understand, but this has to be a *you* thing. Rick will be there to give you a hand getting Molly back." Then he took a moment to add, "Then you have to decide what you want to do."

"What *I* want to do? What does that mean?" Langdon asked.

"Are you coming to work for me?" Terk asked.

Langdon hesitated. "Why would you even want me right now?" he snapped once more. "I can't do a damn thing. I sure as hell can't do any remote viewing or astral walking anymore. … You already know that, don't you?" Such bitterness filled his tone that only dead silence was heard on the other end, almost as if Terk was waiting to see if Langdon had run out of steam yet. "Fine. … I get it. I sound like a damn two-year-old."

At that, Terk laughed out loud. "I'm about to be inundated with babies here, and I was never very good at that whole babysitting thing. However, what I am good at is separating the chaff from the wheat," he stated in a calm tone. "You had what it takes before, and you certainly have it still."

"You wish."

"I know it may sound trite, … lame even," Terk added, "but, until I really understand what the issue is, I can't help you, and you probably realize that yourself anyway. Yet a lot of it is mental, as much as anything."

"Right, I know. I'm already a headcase," he muttered, with a certain amount of bitterness.

Terk smiled, and it easily came through in his tone of voice. "You always *were* a headcase, Langdon," Terk noted with such affection that Langdon had to close his eyes and swear again.

"How the hell did you always know when I was in trouble?" he asked.

"That's what friends are for."

Langdon stopped at that and sighed. "What kind of a friend am I when I won't even come and work for you?"

"Not everybody works well together and remains friends at the same time." Terk chuckled. "Still, I would be remiss if I didn't offer you a job again, particularly now that we're private, plus knowing you're having trouble adapting."

"Didn't it occur to you that it wouldn't be good to hire

me for exactly those reasons? The first thing you learn when you go private is that this is a business and that I'm not a good prospect."

"That's for me to say, not for you to decide without even consulting me," Terkel stated. "I admit I have an awful lot to learn about the business side of things, and so I mostly go by the feel of things because I know no other way to operate."

"Exactly my point. Again not a good way to do business," Langdon repeated.

"But it's my business, so you'll just have to deal with it," Terk replied, with finality. "We'll help you find Molly, and then we'll talk about it again."

"Yeah? What's the price for helping to find Molly though?"

Terk hesitated for a moment. "I'll think about it," he murmured. "Right now, the big thing is getting her back."

"Yeah, but I don't want to be beholden."

"Yep, I got it," Terk noted, "but I think I know who Molly is—energetically."

"So what if you do?" Langdon asked curiously.

"I may want to talk to her myself." And, with that, Terk hung up, leaving Langdon staring at his phone in shock.

That was the thing about Terk. He was always on top of the game. So much so that it was unnerving. They had been friends for a long time but had parted ways years ago. Langdon had gone off to work in the British government, while Terk chose to start working for the CIA.

Though he'd been approached by Terk several times, Langdon found the idea of working for the US government unsettling. Not that he had anything against them personally, but his father and his brother had both worked for the US government, and their stories made Langdon weary of potential antics. He groaned as he sat back, considering the foolish decisions he had made over his life, wondering if he would be whole right now if he had gone to work for Terk back then.

Not that it made a damn bit of difference now because life just didn't work that way. Langdon had made the decision and was now dealing with the fallout. His father had more or less laughed at him when he'd gotten injured and had told him it was his own fault, and he should have been working on their side of the pond the whole time. Not that it made much difference as far as Langdon could tell because the Americans had just as many people coming home with injuries as the Brits did. Still, it was one more little thing in the back of his mind that bothered him. That's when he realized Terk hadn't mentioned where he was working from these days.

Langdon quickly sent him a text, asking what country he was living in and who was he serving now. Terk had mentioned that he'd gone private, but that didn't mean a whole lot.

The response came back almost immediately, saying, they were in Manchester, working privately, doing a certain amount of jobs with MI6 in England, but they were also open to projects elsewhere in the world—but only on the side of right.

Langdon smiled at that because he would have expected no less from Terkel. Langdon hadn't realized he'd needed to hear it, but apparently he did, and any assurance was a saving grace. When a text arrived a few minutes later, followed by an odd knock on the door, Langdon got up slowly and moved toward the door. "Who is it?"

After a moment of silence came the response. "Rick."

Hesitating, not having asked for any images to confirm who was at his door, Langdon opened the peephole first. There he saw a built-up hulk of a man staring back at him, completely calm and at peace with himself. Langdon found himself hating him already. He glared at him. "Yeah. What are you doing here?"

One eyebrow went up slowly. "Terk asked me to come and help you find Molly, presuming that finding Molly is still a priority for you."

Langdon winced at that, then quickly slammed shut the peephole and opened the door. "Yes, finding Molly is a priority," he muttered.

The guy walked in and nodded. "I'm Rick."

"Nice to meet you," Langdon replied with a sigh, pushing his hair off his forehead. "Sorry for the less-than-exuberant welcome." And, with that, he hobbled over to a chair and sat down.

Rick came in beside him, took one look at the leg, and whistled. "Obviously you've been on that too much."

"Ya think? It also wasn't easy to ask for help, but Molly is in trouble, and it's my fault. Thus I gotta do what I gotta do, and the rest of it be damned." He glared down at his leg and specifically where the prosthetic met the inflammation, burning up the puffy surface of the stump.

"How long ago did that happen?" Rick asked.

"Six months. Two surgeries since and it just won't calm down."

"I suppose getting off it and staying off it isn't much of an option," he noted.

Langdon could sense Rick studying him, as he shook his head. "No, it's not an option." Langdon tried hard to keep the bitterness out of his tone. "Molly is missing and may be in grave danger, and I don't have anybody else to call on but Terk."

"You called for help, and I'm here because Terk asked me to come."

Langdon studied him. "Do you work for him?"

"Yes, I work for him. I worked with him when he worked for the CIA as well. Now that we're independent, we all still work together."

Langdon nodded. "I guess that works out okay for you guys?"

At that, Rick smiled. "Honestly, we're still pretty new to it yet, being private and all, but I wouldn't have it any other way."

The quiet joy in his tone made Langdon do a double take. He hesitated before he spoke, not sure how to put it right. "You almost sound like you're … happy."

"I am happy. I'm happier than I ever thought I could be," he admitted, then pointed to Langdon's swollen stump. "When you're in the industry that we're in, that sort of thing can happen at any time. We've certainly had enough accidents and attacks to be mindful that what we do is something we may not recover from. Yet, after we do recover, that feeling of grace comes with the knowledge that we managed to rebuild something much better on the other side. Only then can we start to appreciate what we have. Only when we forget to appreciate what we have does it all go to pot again."

"I hope that you can keep up the cheerleading for yourself when the time comes for you," Langdon replied, his tone almost caustic, "because, if your luck doesn't hold, you end up like this."

"Listen." Rick motioned with his hand. "I get that you

have a chip on your shoulder about it right now, but we came to help. Therefore, if we can do something, maybe you should tune me in to what's going on here."

Langdon stared at him and then groaned. "Look, man. I'm sorry. I'm not intentionally being an ass. Believe me. I recognize that I tend to do it without even trying, but I was doing better. In fact, I thought I was fine, until this all blew up, and now I'm sidelined—at least to some degree." He looked away. "I've been told that if I don't keep somewhat off this leg and take care of this, there's a good chance I'll never wear a prosthetic because I overdid it, … overdid it while trying to find Molly myself. It's not looking good for me, which is why I put in the call for help."

"We've answered," Rick declared, his voice firm and compassionate but definitely not sympathetic. "Now, before you end up getting yourself in deeper, as you just described, why don't you tell me what's going on and how can we help."

Just then came another knock on the door. Rick looked over at him. "You expecting anybody else?"

Langdon immediately shook his head. "No, I'm not expecting anybody, but that doesn't mean much," Langdon replied cautiously. "I don't know who all Terk may have sent."

At that, Rick smiled. "Good point." He opened the door, while Langdon watched, letting somebody else in. As the stranger approached, he looked over, assessed the leg with a wince. "Good thing you called before you lose that leg."

"I'm not losing it." Langdon swore.

"You mean, you're not losing the rest of it."

Langdon glared at the newcomer. "Who are you?"

"I'm Riff. I'm here to help, if I can do something for you," he replied, his tone cheerful and yet hard. "So, don't waste my time, as I won't hang around if you do."

Langdon stared back and forth between the two of them. "Are you all like this?"

"Yep," Rick agreed, "to a certain extent we are. One way or another, we've all been through the grinder ourselves, and wherever we're at in life is because of it."

"All right." Langdon waved his arms. "I get it. ... Whatever." His tone turned harsh, as he eyed both men intently. "The only reason I called for help"—the emotions in his tone revealed how much that request had cost him—"is because I need to confirm that Molly is safe."

"Right, we got it, and we're happy to get down to business," Rick stated.

"Me too," chimed in Riff. "Now give us the details, and let's get to it quickly. How do you even know she's missing? When did she go missing? And, most important, what happened?"

Langdon took a deep breath. "Judge me if you want, but we had a hell of a fight. She took off on me, and, given that she has abilities of her own, ... she's always been extremely, let's call it, self-sufficient. I was wallowing in self-pity," he admitted, then stopped and winced. "I was a mess. But recently my adoptive mother was killed in a home invasion. Molly is her caretaker, so obviously I worried about her safety. Once I realized she wasn't out there—answering in any way that I could see—I really got worried. I made a bunch of phone calls and found out that nobody had seen or heard from her recently. I went to her apartment and didn't find anything of note there either. I have a key, if you want to check it out yourselves."

Langdon got up, using a cane, and hobbled over to a counter, where he grabbed a key off the ring and handed it over to Riff, along with the address. "From that point, I don't know any more, except that I got a text from her, saying not to worry and that she was fine."

"What was it about that text that set off the alarms?"

"She would never say something like that. She absolutely hates it when she has to tell people she's fine, and, between us, it's a big issue for her," he murmured. "It's just not the way she would word it. She probably would have said something more like, 'I hope you die,' or maybe, 'Go jump off the closest bridge,' something along those lines," he shared, with a wry look. "That would be more her style."

"How long have you known her?"

"We were an item until my accident. The problem came after …" He pointed at the stump. "I was really struggling. She wanted me to get some extra help, and I wasn't ready or willing to do it, and it went downhill between us from there. She'd stepped up to help my mother, who needed more care than she would admit, to but didn't want nurses around whom I sent over during the day. However, my mother's diabetes was out of hand, and her feet kept her immobile most of the time. Then she was murdered by a goddamned druggie, who broke in, looking for something to sell. Amazingly Molly nor the nurses were there at the time or others could have been killed too. The intruder, high as a kite, shot my mother when she sat up in bed. Molly works freelance and yet was taking on my mother too, like a second job. Even though we broke up, Molly was there for me, then and now," he muttered. "So, yeah, go ahead and blame me. I don't really care. I just need to know that Molly's okay. All that matters is that she's safe."

Riff sent Langdon a long, hard look. "You really think she's in danger? Better yet, if you really think so, my next question would be why."

Langdon winced. "I have a few abilities, but all that has gone sideways since my injury. I can't trust my abilities," he stated bluntly. "What I can trust is the fact that Molly screamed out in the night—maybe two days ago, I guess—and she was screaming at me to help. I couldn't even get a location, couldn't get anything from her on it. She has been silent ever since."

"When you say you have or had abilities, what does that mean?" Rick asked.

Langdon shrugged. "I used to have a locator beam," he shared. "Something that would give me a sense of direction, … if we should go left or right, something like that. If we were out in the field or hunting, it would give me a tracking beam. Obviously that explanation is probably not much help, and there are certainly other avenues to it, but the bottom line is, I don't even seem to have that anymore."

"Do you know why?"

"No, I don't," he lied bluntly, but seeing the looks on their faces, Langdon knew they knew better. He sighed. "I have a couple ideas, but nothing I am prepared to disclose just yet. The *why* part of it still eludes me. I know a lot of that is due to my accident, my injury, and all kinds of things that have been whacked out since then. I don't feel very normal since the last surgery. In fact, the last surgery really did a number on me."

"How long ago was that?" Rick asked.

He stopped, thought about it. "A week, maybe ten days. I was on pretty heavy-duty painkillers. Then I got a prosthetic to try and went over to Molly's place, and it hurt the stump some more," he muttered, looking down at his leg. "I'm not immobile, but I'm not exactly what you would call agile either."

"No, you're definitely not mobile," Rick confirmed, with a nod. "I'll start by heading over to her place and see what I can find."

"While we're doing that," Riff stated, getting to his feet, facing Langdon, "you start a list of who might want to hurt her. Make sure to remember every little detail as to why she could be targeted. Rack your brain for what she does for work, whether work would have anything to do with it, friends, exes, the whole nine yards."

"I have been trying to think of things like that," Langdon muttered, "but so far I'm running on empty."

Then Rick turned toward Langdon, just as Rick reached the doorway. "Add to that list anybody who you think would try to get to her because of you."

"What do you mean?" Langdon asked, startled.

"Who hates you enough that they would take Molly as leverage or maybe even to cause you maximum pain?" Rick asked. He gave him a clipped nod and walked out.

MOLLY TWISTED AGAINST the bindings on her wrists, cursing herself for not having watched the videos always popping up on YouTube and on other platforms, showing how to get out of restraints like this. It seemed like there always were tricks, but the movements were particular and precise. She tried, based on what she remembered, but none of it seemed to apply to her situation right now.

She could only hope that there was some way to do it,

but her mind came up blank, and that was hurting her more than anything. The tears had long since dried, along with the moisture in her throat. At this point, it was hard for her to even swallow, and the gag itself was made of some fibrous material that kept tickling her throat. It seemed that, if she were to take it off, she would immediate seize up with a coughing fit. Maybe that would be the best thing for it. She didn't know at this point in time, and it was just so frustrating. Meanwhile she kept sending messages to Langdon, hoping against hope that he would still receive them, but he could be beyond stubborn. Then again she was here because she was also stubborn.

If she hadn't walked out, the two of them would be doing much better at life. Even if they weren't together, they would still be doing better. She continued to blame herself for the breakup, as she should have given him more time to process what had happened to his leg. Hell, she needed that too. Since she'd walked, he'd basically built a wall between them of nonnegotiable terms. She couldn't really blame him, given the hard place he was in right now. He wouldn't let just anybody in to help. And she knew that blaming herself wouldn't do any good either. It sure as heck wouldn't get her out of this nightmare.

Her kidnapper hadn't asked anything of her. He had come in, had taken off her gag, and had given her water, which she'd sucked down greedily, but then immediately the gag was put back on, and he walked out. Now she needed to go to the bathroom something awful, and her throat was full of this fiber, and she was struggling to breathe. All in all, everything had begun to terrify her. She hadn't really expected to die today—or a few days ago, when she was taken—and it still wasn't among her plans. She just wasn't sure that everyone else felt the same way, and that made her beyond sad. She had hoped that her life at this stage would be so different, so unique, extraordinary even, and she felt as if she'd failed at every turn.

She wasn't even sure that it was her fault, not that there had to be fault assigned, but, by not having succeeded at her goals, it felt as if she had missed out on something major. She knew she had wanted to be extraordinary with Langdon, but that last surgery had done something to him, and she didn't think he recognized the changes it had brought.

She wanted to talk to him about it and had tried several times, but he just wasn't open to hearing anything. She had to say that it was mostly him, his own insecurities. However, she hadn't been easy on him either and had given him hell. Now that may well have been something he fully deserved but probably wasn't ready to hear. She, on the other hand, was out of patience but hadn't chosen the time for her tough love routine with any great finesse either.

Plus, he was now dealing with the recent loss of his mother too. She hadn't been able to speak to him since that had happened.

Now, here she was, captive and potentially never getting an opportunity to change things. The door opened suddenly, and she found herself staring up at the same man as before. He undid the gag around her mouth, and she immediately started coughing, trying to get rid of the fibers still in her throat. She glared at him, as she whispered, "There are fibers on your gag. They're choking me."

He shrugged. "Like I care."

Her glare deepened. "Presumably you're doing this for money or something, and, if I die, it's all for naught," she pointed out. "So, you might want to keep that in mind."

He gave her an ugly grin. "I don't give a crap if you live or die," he declared cheerfully. "Still, a few people think you can bring them something they want pretty badly."

Her gaze sharpened. "I think they are wrong."

"You better hope they're not," he replied sarcastically. "Otherwise your life isn't worth keeping, and I, for one, would prefer not to babysit someone so useless and pathetic." He quickly undid the ties on her ankles and handed her a bottle of water. She sucked back on the water greedily, until he plucked the bottle from her hands. "I wouldn't keep doing that if I were you. I won't take you to the bathroom all the time just because you need to go."

She stared at him. "I do need to go."

"That's why I'm here. So quit your bellyaching, and let's go."

She pinched her lips together, desperately trying to get along because her options didn't appear to be great. Still, she wanted to smack him. He was a lumbering 250, 260 pounds easily, not tall, but he was squat. That force, the balance of gravity, was at such a point that she didn't think she could knock him over anyhow. She had worked her way through multiple colors of belts in her pursuit of martial arts, but, even then, she wasn't so sure.

On the other hand, he was cocky. He had no weapon, and he didn't seem to think she posed any kind of a threat, and that in itself angered her. Molly wanted somebody to at least think twice before they kidnapped her, but apparently she hadn't even been worthy of that.

With that thought came the very sobering reminder that the world out there didn't operate on the same values that she had cultivated—if they even gave a crap about having values at all, something else that saddened her tremendously.

Stumbling to her feet, she almost fell as the blood rushed down past her ankles that had been tied up in a weird position the whole time.

She cried out, but he jerked her forward roughly. "Make a sound again," he uttered, his tone quiet and lethal, "and I'll see that you don't get a chance to make another ... ever."

She stared up at him, mute.

He dragged her forward, out of the room and into the hallway and down to the bathroom. The door was open and didn't seem to even close properly. He motioned at her. "No funny stuff."

She stared at him. "You will turn your back, won't you?"

He gave her a flat smile and replied scathingly, "No." Frowning, she went into the small room, looked around, and he barked behind her, "Hurry up, or I'm taking you back, and you can piss yourself. I really don't care."

Hating him more every time he opened his mouth, plus doing her best to retain a modicum of privacy, she sat down on the toilet and emptied her bladder. When she was done, she looked around for toilet paper but found none. He snorted, grabbed something off the shelf at the other side and tossed her a roll. Again keeping herself covered as much as she could, she finished the job and stood to hit the flusher. She gingerly walked over to the sink, which was nasty and rusted. If she were lucky, it would still pour out water, but she wouldn't count on it. She quickly turned it on, just in case her captor wouldn't give her the chance to wash her hands.

As soon as she held out her hands, it poured.

He walked to the sink and shut it off a moment later. "That's enough. I don't want you thinking this is some five-star hotel." Then he cracked up, laughing, as if it was the funniest joke ever.

She didn't say anything, but, with her bladder now empty and some water for her throat, she felt better.

She quickly glanced around the small room but nothing here to see. Even as she stepped into the hallway, it was empty, nothing to grab to tell anybody where she was. By the time she was back in her small room, and he had tied her up again, and she had no more information as to where she was than she did before.

She faced him and asked, "Do you really need to tie me up? It's not as if I can go anywhere." He frowned at her, and she pleaded, "I would really appreciate no gag at least. Honestly the fibers are coming loose on that cloth." He looked down at it and saw that it was obviously frayed, with material shredding everywhere.

"Fine," he replied, bored and tired, "but I'm giving you one and only one warning. If you make any attempt to come up to that door, I'll flatten you so fast that it'll break your jaw, and then I'll really go to town and break your legs." With that he stepped out, leaving her trembling in his wake.

Thankful that she could breathe more easily, she crawled on the dirt floor into the corner and immediately sent out telepathic messages to anybody who could hear them. But when they all bounced back to her, she realized that her secret weapon, the one thing she had hoped would do something for her, was a no-show.

Her one chance at freedom failed her, and she couldn't imagine how that could be. It wouldn't work for whatever reason. It was quite possibly because of her location, but, if that were the case, she must be underground in a steel or concrete-encased building, where nothing she could do mentally would come in or out, and that was the final straw.

She hated cry-baby women, but, if anybody had a reason

to cry, it was Molly right now. She felt the hot tears well up and roll down her cheeks. She had no idea how she was supposed to get a message out to anybody who could even find her. Getting a message out was one thing, but having anybody reach her and come to save her was a completely different problem.

Yet the person she knew to be most capable of handling it was Langdon. And not only was he not listening, chances were, he wouldn't get past all this concrete either. For better or for worse, she was stuck here, currently at the whim of this man, who wouldn't even explain what she was doing here or why.

As a matter of fact, he hadn't said anything that made any sense so far. That in itself was even more bothersome. The only thing he'd mentioned so far was that she would find out soon, and she could only imagine that he was waiting for somebody to arrive. It was the *who* that terrified her. She didn't know very many people in this world, and nobody that she worked with at her freelancing job knew anything about her abilities. They never knew about her other job as caretaker for Langdon's mom either. It would be far too dangerous to let the world know about her abilities or Langdon's abilities. She was really hoping her kidnapping had nothing to do with her, but figured that she probably wasn't anywhere near as lucky as that.

Her whole life had been one of attracting bad luck. While everybody else was winning the family lottery or the boyfriend lottery or the children lottery or whatever lottery was out there, Molly was in this firm *fail* category each and every time. This time she'd really hoped that maybe somebody out there would save her, but, so far, it looked to be a complete dead end.

Once again that didn't surprise her, but she could hope.

CHAPTER 2

WHEN THE DOOR opened, Molly woke with a start. She was dragged roughly to her feet, led to the bathroom, and it was the same deal as before. The only difference, instead of taking her back to the same room while she was still groggy and trying to shake off the sleep, she was led to another room and parked on a chair. She sat quietly, waiting for whomever to show his hand. When somebody stepped into the room, took one look at her, and laughed, it was her time to be dumbfounded. She stared at him in disbelief.

"Arthur?" She was stunned, but, as soon as the shock left her, it was replaced by a seething anger. She knew him. Why would he do this to her?

He laughed again. "God, you're pathetic," he muttered. "Look at you."

She stared at him. "It's not as if I have much choice at the moment."

"No, you sure don't," he agreed, "but then again, you shouldn't have spurned me quite like you did."

She frowned at him and shook her head. "Is that what this is about?"

He shot her a look of complete contempt. "No, I wouldn't touch that psycho body of yours no matter what," he muttered. "I just thought it might be easier to get some information from you this way."

"I don't have any information to give," she replied, puzzled. She knew Arthur as a contractor for the company she worked for, at least she thought he did. "What is this all about?"

He looked at her, then shook his head. "You really don't get it, do you?"

At the sake of being called stupid or God-only-knows what other insults he had planned for her, she shook her head. "No, I really don't."

"Of course you don't," he stated in disgust. "It always blew me away that he was so sure that you were the one for him, while you were so sure that he was the one for you. Yet, I wonder, … since here you are, and you don't even know what he was doing in life."

"I don't know what you're talking about," she admitted, confused. "*Who* are you talking about?" Arthur continued to stare at her, as she shook her head. "The only person who even makes any sense … is Langdon."

"Yeah, bully for you," he stated, with a snort. "You finally got there."

"No," she disagreed, "I haven't gotten anywhere because I don't have anything at all to do with Langdon."

"Yet you wished you did," he shouted. "That's one of the things I had to come to terms with. You're just a wannabe."

"I want to be what?" she asked, staring at him in shock.

He glared at her. "Listen. I need something from Langdon," he began, finally cutting to the chase. "He has an ability, a skill that I need."

Her gaze widened, but her heart sank. "What are you talking about?"

Arthur shrugged. "Obviously I would have preferred it was you, but you're completely useless in that department, but, considering how very specialized he is, that makes more sense," he muttered. "Still, I had hoped."

"You had hoped what?" she asked, shaking her head. "What kind of skill? He's ex-military, sure. What more do you need?"

"Yep, he's military," Arthur confirmed, with a small nod. "British military."

She nodded slowly. "You want something from the British military?" she asked in a hazy voice.

"No, … not likely, but they do have some interesting aces up their sleeves."

She just shook her head because none of this made any sense at all.

He laughed again. "It doesn't matter. Clearly you don't know anything about it, so you are useless, outside of the fact that Langdon cares about what happens to you."

"No," she replied, "Langdon *cared* about what happened to me at one time, but we've been broken up for a while, and he certainly wants nothing to do with me now."

That stopped Arthur in his tracks. "Seriously?"

She nodded.

"Why is that?"

"He's different since his last surgery," she muttered. "Angry, not, … not the same at all. And I … pushed him."

"Of course you did." Arthur snorted. "Something women are so damn good at. You can't keep your mouth shut, and you push a guy when he's already down on his luck. That surgery was brutal. Plus that doctor basically told him that he won't even get a prosthetic, and there you are, pushing him. Jesus."

"What do you mean, he won't get a prosthetic?" she asked, puzzled. "He just had the surgery so he could get a prosthetic."

"Yeah, as long as he doesn't do anything to irritate his stump," Arthur clarified, "but, of course, he's already done that. Plus some of that work he was doing, ... it didn't do him any good. So I was hoping that, by taking you, I would push him over the edge. He wouldn't get a prosthetic for sure, and why should he have a prosthetic or even a life past this? When he gets to feeling that way, he'll be right where I want him and willing to talk."

"Why would he be willing to talk?" she asked.

"To save your life, for starters."

She sighed. "That might have worked in the past, but now? ... No way."

"Oh, you better hope it still works," Arthur snapped, his tone turning ugly, "because otherwise I have absolutely no use for having you here and putting up with you. And, if you're of no use to me, believe me. I'll just ditch you on the wayside the first chance I get. Then again, you wouldn't be alive to care anyway."

Her eyes widened at that.

"I can't exactly leave you around telling tales, can I?" She swallowed hard, and he laughed again. "Yeah, I see you're finally getting the picture."

"I'm getting something," she muttered. "I just don't understand ... *why?* What is this all about?"

"It doesn't matter if you understand or not. All I need is Langdon. And you? ... You're just a means to an end."

"What is it that you want from him?" she asked curiously.

"That skill of his. That's what I need."

"So, you want him to go to work for you?" she asked, starting with an educated guess. "You think that he would do it for me? So, it's some kind of work that he won't want to do without this kind of pressure?"

"He's already turned me down several times," Arthur said, with a smile, "but, this way, he won't be able to."

"Ah, I see. So contact him then and find out if he will or not because this is not exactly the easiest way to live."

He looked at her. "Oh, are you already complaining about your accommodations? I'm so sorry." His tone was cruel and mocking.

She knew he wasn't sorry in the least. It didn't exactly help, but, as long as she kept the conversation going, hopefully he wasn't planning her murder. *Yet.* She just waited for him to say something else.

"Anyway, until I have a chance to connect with him and to give him my demands, you will be our guest."

She didn't say anything more and just waited.

"What? Nothing to say?"

She shrugged. "Nothing I can say. You have made that pretty clear. So, while it would be nice if the accommodations were a little better, I don't think that's at the top of your list."

"No, it isn't." Arthur sneered at her. "We'll keep you locked up. I don't mind if the gag comes off, but do you see Bingo over here?" He pointed out the guard at the door, who waved at her. "If Bingo hears you scream or cry out or in any way sees you try to escape, I don't have a problem with him setting you back on your heels to get your attention. Got it?"

She nodded. "Got it." And no matter how badly she itched to say more, she did get it. That Bingo guy looked a little too much like he was ready for some punching bag exercise, and punching her was probably right up his alley.

With that, she was motioned to her feet and led back to her room. When she was pushed to the dirt floor, she crawled up in the corner once again to get away from Bingo and curled up. Once she was alone, she tried to reach out, but nobody was there. Just walls all around her, thick, heavy walls. Walls that she had absolutely no hope of getting through.

She pondered what Arthur had told her and then wondered if Langdon's psychic abilities were what Arthur had referred to. That had to be it. You could hire people with all kinds of military backgrounds, but Langdon's abilities for tracking were truly unique, not that Langdon had really spent much time developing them, but they were part and parcel of the work that he did for the government.

He never really did anything to advertise these energy gifts, so how would Arthur even know? If Arthur wanted that special tracking ability, what did he want Langdon to find? That would be a whole different story because no way in hell would Langdon get pushed into using those abilities under duress, particularly since she was pretty sure that part of the reason he was so miserable was the fact that his abilities had disappeared after his latest surgery.

She just didn't know whether that was the truth or if something else was involved. She'd wanted to talk to him about it many times, but he'd always shut her down. Then she'd pushed it, and he then shut them both down. *Yay* for being stupid, but that's what happened when you cared for someone. You pushed the lines, and sometimes made a misjudgment by doing so. Now, if you were lucky and if you had a chance, you could pull back long enough to maintain the relationship, but if you did what Molly did and continued to push, then he ended up where he was, and she ended up out in the cold.

Now she had to see what Arthur would do to her.

AS SOON AS Riff and Rick disappeared, Langdon sat down again and started sending out messages, looking for Molly. He had never really explored the kind of energy work he did, but somehow he and Molly had connected on a telepathic level, and he'd been trying to reopen that damn door for weeks—ever since he'd slammed it shut when she got too pushy. He'd done it in a fit of anger, but that was a damn mistake. He hadn't been quite ready to share just then. Now all he could do was regret that. He needed to contact her, to explain why he wasn't there and couldn't come to her rescue, and to let her know that, if she could do anything for herself, she needed to do it because this was looking like a bad deal all around.

Although he didn't have any proof that she was in a serious situation, his heart knew it. If his heart knew it, his instincts were screaming it too, and … he was never wrong. He'd known when his mother would die. He'd known when his brother had gotten into a severe car accident, and the list went on and on. Just too many times that knowledge held him in good stead, even though the bearer of bad news.

And now he knew perfectly well that Molly was in trouble. How he would have managed to explain it to Riff and Rick, Langdon didn't know. But the fact was, they were all part of Terk's team, and that most likely meant that they had abilities of their own. At that, Terk popped into his head.

They absolutely do, he murmured, *but, if you know any-*

thing that can help them find Molly, you need to tell them.

"I wish I could," he snapped, "and I'm already doing as much as I can."

I know you are, Terk noted, his voice calm. *Yet you could do more, but first you need to ditch that anger.*

"She's missing because of me," he grumbled, grating his teeth.

I gather that she's missing because she walked away after a fight with you, and that much is true. Did you have anything physically to do with her disappearance?

"No, of course not," Langdon snapped.

Then she's not missing because of you. Molly's missing because of the asshole who took her.

"What if it is because of me?"

Then we deal with it, Terk murmured. *We won't jump ahead and get into any kind of blame game at the moment. No time or energy for that.*

So very much like Terk to calmly sit back and relax, while things were in progress. Until they got actual intel, no point in getting too emotional. "I love her, you know," Langdon whispered. At that admission, he felt Terk smile.

I know you do. Why do you think I'm here for you? She has to be a very special woman, if you care that much.

"Yeah, … she is very special. That's why I sent her away."

After a pause on the other end, Terk laughed. *If I had a dollar for every time I've heard a strong man say something like that about the woman he loved, I would be very rich. Everybody always thinks these women would be better off without them.*

"It's true," Langdon argued. "You don't understand."

No, I sure don't, Terk agreed in a nonchalant tone. *But, if you're not six feet under the ground, I am here to tell you that she won't understand either.*

Langdon groaned. "I was thinking that maybe, with time, she would. That she'd find somebody else and move on."

Nope, not happening, Terk shared, with a chuckle. *She'll just get angrier, and then she will cause some kind of commotion that brings this all to a head, and then you'll have to deal with it.*

"Yeah, well, that's already happened," Langon muttered. "I had to send her away. I had no other choice."

And she went? Just like that? Terk asked in amazement.

"Yeah." Langdon pondered that. "Although I suspect it was just to reinforce her own beliefs and to figure out another plan of attack."

Good, then that's more like the woman I was expecting.

"Why?" he asked.

For one, you've never been easy to get along with. You've always been stubborn, and you've always thought you knew what was right.

"I do," Langdon agreed bleakly. "It's much better than being in a relationship with half a man."

You say that, but consider how she would look at that, Terk suggested, trying to reason with him. *I have to tell you though, that my views on women and what they will and will not tolerate have changed somewhat in recent times,* Terk admitted, with a half chuckle.

"Yeah? So what are you, some sort of specialist on women now?" Langdon asked, challenging Terk.

Oh, I wouldn't say that at all. I don't think my wife would either.

"Wife?" Langdon repeated in amazement.

Yeah, wife.

"And Rick?"

He's got a partner too. We have another team member on his way to you, but he's been held up, so I'm not sure when he'll arrive. So, if a man called Eton shows up, be nice to him. He's there to help.

"What about Riff?"

Now Riff is a whole different story. No matter what happens, do us both a favor and don't go shake that tiger's tail.

"What's the story with Riff?" Langdon asked suspiciously.

His fiancée was murdered and, part of the deal for him working for us, is that we're trying to track down what happened.

"Well, shit," Langdon muttered, stunned.

Yeah, so you see? It's not just your life that's in the sewer, Terk shared, his voice soft. *I do understand that, from your perspective, it seems that way, but it's not.*

"Yeah, *great,*" Langdon grumbled. "I don't want any empathy from these guys. None of us ever do, because it hurts. It hurts that most of us aren't capable of opening up about it. That used to be you too."

Yes, until I opened up, Terk explained. *And I found out that there was an awful lot more to life than being alone all the damn time and that just because we felt that the women couldn't handle what we do, it didn't mean that we were right. Believe me. I've paid for that a time or two.*

At that, Langdon burst out laughing. "She must be pretty special, if she can handle you."

She's very special all right, and, yes, she can handle me, Terk replied, with a note of humor. *And, by the way, we're expecting twins.*

That startled a laugh out of Langdon, which then rolled

into long chuckles. "Oh my God, seriously?"

Yeah, seriously, and, before you rant on, it wasn't something I expected. I didn't ask for it, and I never went looking for it, but right now? I couldn't imagine my life any other way, he murmured. *So maybe you should give Molly a chance.*

"Yeah, I should," Langdon agreed, sobering, "and, if I ever get an opportunity to tell her, I'll have a talk with her. I promise."

Now see? Your success will depend on if you have a talk with her or if you give her that chance, Terk added.

"I need to know where she is," Langdon argued.

Can I just say that the powers that be would be a whole lot more amiable if you weren't such an ass.

"I've been an ass nonstop," he muttered. "It will be a little hard to change now."

Maybe so, Terk noted, *but think about it. Nothing like learning to grovel, while you have the opportunity to win Molly back.*

Langdon snorted. "I don't even think groveling will make a difference."

Depends what's been done to her in the meantime, Terk pointed out.

At that, Langdon sucked in his breath, feeling the pain in his heart. "If they've touched her, I don't give a shit how many limbs I have to lose. You know I'll take them down."

I know. Terk understood Langdon very clearly. *So let's just find Molly. Let's figure out what's going on with her kidnapper, and we'll go from there,* and, with that, Terk disappeared from Langdon's head.

The fact that he could even still talk to Terk telepathically revealed a lot about Terk's abilities. It didn't say much for Langdon's, but Terk had always been exceptional when it came to everybody else in this world. He was that one person who could do things others couldn't even imagine—and do so with ease. Terk was the kind of guy who could do things on the other side of energy work that most people never even had a chance to think about, let alone practice or try, yet he did it effortlessly.

It was one of the things that people either loved or hated about Terk and his team, and there was no two ways with Terk. He was a good man, always accountable, always on the side of right. Langdon had never had a problem with Terk himself, except for the fact that he'd always tried to get Langdon to work for the CIA. At that thought, Terk was in his head again.

Yeah, well, … we're private now. Remember that.

"Yeah, I'm trying to," Langdon muttered. "It's still not exactly something I can get my mind wrapped around."

Don't have to get wrapped around anything at the moment, Terk stated. *First we find Molly. Then maybe I should talk to her.*

"Why?"

You can talk to her telepathically, can't you?

"Yes, I used to be able to," Langdon muttered. "Right now? … It's not working, and I'm not getting anything, but then, in my state, I haven't got any messages from her for a very long time."

Interesting, Terk said. *That would be something to research.*

"And what? Any doctors would probably just tell me it came from the surgeries or the anesthesia or something."

My entire team was attacked not long ago, Terk began, *and I have to tell you. In most cases, they came back better and stronger than ever. So, if that might happen to you as well, it's something you could look forward to.*

"If that's even possible," Langdon argued. "I'm not sure I believe it. Who would be the one to do that kind of research?" he asked curiously.

At that, Terk laughed. *You should meet my wife*, he replied affectionately. *It's one of the reasons we met. She was doing research on paranormal abilities.*

Langdon was shocked and couldn't believe it. "You talked to her? Telepathically?"

Not really talked to her at first, he replied coyly. *It's a long story, but, at the end of the day, we made it, so it doesn't really matter.*

"That sounds like a story I might be interested in hearing."

Oh, yeah, you absolutely will, Terk agreed. *When this is over, we'll have you both over, and you can come meet everybody.*

"*Hmm*, that sounds strange, coming from you. It sounds like, you know, being sociable."

Yeah, I know it's a stretch, Terk teased, chuckling, *but you can do it.*

"I haven't been social in a while."

I know. That stage of life is pretty rough.

"It is, indeed. At this point there's a good chance I won't have a prosthetic."

Before you give up on that, you need to contact somebody in New Mexico. There may still be someone who can help.

"Yeah, I've heard about that woman before," Langdon said, "but it's not like I can get in to see her. One, I don't know that she would even take me on, and two, I'm over here across the pond."

I'm pretty sure she would take you on as a special favor and at least take a look, but you're right. No guarantee she could do anything for you, but she has got abilities in that specialty, like you wouldn't believe.

"So I've heard, yet found hard to believe," he admitted grudgingly. "I haven't contacted her. I just assumed she probably has a massive waiting list."

Potentially, though I'm not sure that she gives a crap about it. As far as I know, Kat's working with all kinds of people, several I know quite well.

"Interesting." Though Langdon hated to admit it, a tiny flicker of interest and even hope bloomed in his heart. "According to the doctors here, the damage is too severe, and I can't put any weight on it."

As far as that goes, Terk replied, *I also have some pretty incredible healers on staff.*

"Healers?" Langdon asked cautiously.

Yeah, paranormal healers. Some really great energy workers.

Langdon didn't even know what to say to that. "As in real ones?"

Absolutely. Terk laughed. *They would be pretty insulted to be called anything less than that.*

"Jesus, and what … They can heal things?"

They can do all kinds of stuff. Again, I can't give you any confirmation as to what they could or couldn't do with you at the moment because they would need to see you or at least check your energy. So, if you give me permission, I can have one of them take a look.

"How will you do that?" Langdon asked in exasperation, "I'm over here in London. Remember?"

They don't need to be physically where you are, Terk noted. *They can take a look from where they are.*

At that, Langdon stopped, took a deep breath. "Jesus,

you're serious, aren't you?"

Yeah, and it sounds like you've been alone way too long.

Langdon winced. "I *have* been alone for a long time. Is it that obvious?"

Yeah, Terk confirmed. *You've hidden in your cave and pushed everybody away. That's not a good thing, Langdon.*

"I push really well," he muttered. "Besides, *I* might have reached out but *you* answered."

Yes, because I knew you needed help. Although, the more I think about it, I also heard from someone else.

"What do you mean?"

I heard screams from a woman but her energy was connected to you.

"But that must have been Molly," Langdon snapped, bounding to his feet, only to gasp in pain as he struggled to stay upright. "Goddammit," he swore.

Yeah, moving fast won't help, Terk muttered.

"Whatever," Langdon grumbled, "it sounds like Molly has been calling out."

Yes, although I'm not exactly sure where I heard it. I've been doing an awful lot of deep work lately, and it hasn't been the easiest to sort through the layers on the ethers.

"As in … Never mind," Langdon said. "Damn, I'd forgotten how much odd stuff you were into."

Not even odd stuff, Terk corrected calmly. *My abilities continue to develop, with seemingly no end in sight.*

"Damn, I miss that," Langdon muttered.

Of course you do. That's part of being alone all the time, out in the cold, with nobody to help you, or to even be with you. It's not good to isolate yourself to the point that you don't have anybody to bounce ideas and thoughts off of, not to mention nobody for you to develop with, Terk noted, trying really hard to make his point. *That second part is very important in our world.*

"Yet most of us are loners because we don't have anybody else who understands that part of our world."

Exactly, which is another reason for you to come in out of the cold, Terk stated.

Langdon winced at that. "It sounds good and all."

Terk laughed. *You mean, it sounds good and all*, but …

"Yeah, *but*. But I'm not sure you even know what you're talking about anymore."

Ah, of course not, Terk noted, with a chuckle. *You think that, if I knew the truth, I wouldn't even be talking to you, right?*

"Jesus, I hate it when you do that," Langdon muttered. "You don't understand, Terk. I'm different now, since my surgery. Something happened."

I heard you say that your abilities have disappeared, right?

"Exactly, and, if I don't have those abilities, I feel—" He stopped because he didn't even know how to say it.

Let me guess, Terk offered. *Damaged, incomplete, only half of what you were.*

"Yes," Langdon admitted, scrubbing his face. "Like half a man, you know?"

I do know, Terk agreed. *Part of the incident when my team was attacked all at once involved CIA moles. With a chemical machine, they wiped out our abilities. It was a huge mess. Nearly all of us have just gone through exactly what you're talking about.*

"Shit," Langdon replied, yet he also understood that there could be a light at the end of this. "What did you do? How did you get them back?"

Slow down, tiger. In our case, it took time in healing and all that. A couple of my team were lost in the ethers for quite a while. Some were comatose for weeks, but slowly everybody eventually came back online, each in their own time.

"Not the same thing as what I'm going through then," Langdon muttered.

I'm not saying that, Terk noted. *But, beyond your healing, which is a major part of this, you will get better. Now, back to the matter at hand. I need to connect more dots and gaps of information about Molly.*

"What did you find?"

We ran a background check. I don't see any family, and I'm not seeing much in the way of income. What's going on with that?

"She has no family. She would say that she lost a lot around one big event. Her father murdered both her mother and her sister. Molly was an infant at the time, and he thought he'd killed her too, but she ended up in the hospital instead. She was there for several months and has some scars she has mostly outgrown, but mentally and emotionally it's a whole different story. She works as a freelance journalist and hates banks, so she generally keeps her funds in cash at home."

A journalist, huh?

"But not hard news and definitely not crime. She writes about home decor and fashion trends, that kind of stuff. She was looking at going back to school but hadn't got that far. Basically I think she's been waiting for me to get my shit together."

That sounds possible. Terk chuckled. *And, if she doesn't have any enemies in her world, are you hearing or seeing any enemies in yours? ... Specifically anyone who would want to hurt her to get to you?*

"That's what I was trying to do after your two men just left," Langdon shared. "While your guys were gone, they suggested I look into my possible enemies, but I just don't see it, outside of someone hurting her to get at me."

So, who wants to get at you?

"I have no idea," he admitted. "I've worked for the military and traveled all over the place. So, unless somebody has found my face, part of my team, or something on one of these jobs I've been on, I don't really have any personal enemies. But otherwise, sure, it's possible."

Why you though? Why not the rest of your team? Have you contacted any of your other team members to see if they're alive or have been contacted by anybody looking for you?

"No, I haven't, but that's not a bad idea, so maybe not a bad place to start."

Doesn't matter that you fell out of touch. You and I both know that sometimes those memories go way back.

"Okay, fine. I'll sit down and do some work on that."

Yeah, do that, Terk stated. *I'll see if I can reach Molly.*

"How?"

I'll try to follow her energy signature. I tried once, but I didn't get anywhere.

"Yeah, we used to have a door open between us," Langdon shared, "I shut it but she locked it tight."

Ouch, Terk replied in a sobering tone. *Not a good time for that.*

"No, probably the worst."

CHAPTER 3

MOLLY COULDN'T EVEN begin to imagine what nightmare she had gotten herself into or even a plausible way to get out of it. The fact that she had locked the door between her and Langdon was another huge issue, and not so much because she had locked it but it couldn't be reopened unless they both agreed, which was a whole different story.

It was next to impossible because Langdon wouldn't open it. He didn't even know she was in trouble. She had gotten herself into this mess all on her own, and, as much as she liked to think she could get out of it that way, she didn't see it happening very easily or very soon either. She didn't have anything to offer these guys, particularly not money, if that was what they were after, and neither did she have anything along the line of information or skills that they could possibly want.

It bothered her to think that Langdon had energy skills that she didn't know about. Yet all she could really think about were his psychic abilities. When he found out that's what Arthur and Bingo wanted, Langdon would go ballistic. He was completely against using his skills for personal reasons, which is what caused their fight the last time, and now she realized how badly she had underestimated how sensitive he was about it, never dreaming he would completely walk away from her. Talk about learning the hard way. She really had.

She scrubbed at her face, wishing desperately for a shower and a mattress or anything that would make her captivity a little more comfortable. Yet she knew her comfort wasn't the issue here. She didn't have a clue when Arthur and Bingo would get around to contacting Langdon or if they had already done so.

It's quite possible that they had. and he was like, *Yeah, not interested.* But, no, she knew in her heart of hearts that Langdon would never react that way. They had too much history between them.

At the same time, she couldn't imagine a worse scenario that she could have gotten herself into, especially considering the way she and Langdon had parted. It had already been months and months, so if Arthur was hoping to use her for leverage, it would be pretty weak. She and Langdon had had no contact since their breakup, other than her telepathically nagging at him after his latest surgery. Therefore, she had to wonder what kind of leverage she would need to get herself out of this alive. Was there anything left between her and Langdon, or was it a case of too little, too late?

That was always possible, but it wasn't something she was really prepared to look at right now. Not yet. If she got desperate enough, she would do anything to save her life, as anybody would, but she didn't want to throw Langdon to the wolves. She didn't need this mess, but he didn't either. He was dealing with enough crap right now.

Of course Arthur was counting on Langdon caring enough about Molly to save her, and her kidnappers made that first calculation. The second was picking her up. Absolutely no way for her to communicate with Langdon and to let him know, so the kidnappers really planned her abduction well. Aside from Arthur contacting Langdon, she wasn't sure how the hell she was supposed to get out of this. Even if Arthur offered a ransom, if it was something Langdon couldn't do or wouldn't morally do, she had no doubt that would put her in the hot seat.

Even if Langdon wanted to help, he might not be able to on a physical level, or even on a psychic level. And given how Bingo had been, the last time she saw him, she saw absolutely no give in the guy. She wondered if Arthur or Bingo had been a friend of Langdon's in the past. As she thought about it, that made more sense because, if either of them knew about Langdon's energy abilities, that could potentially be the reason for the push to get his assistance.

Langdon had probably turned them down in the past, and now there was absolutely no way to get him to budge, without this kind of added pressure. Though this kind of pressure would only make Langdon even angrier. She could only hope that maybe he didn't hate her completely, and thus he would step up and help out.

With the constant musings running through her head, still wondering how badly she'd burned the bridges behind her and how badly things were in Langdon's world, Molly couldn't do anything but sit here and stew, and it was driving her nuts.

When the door opened, and her guard stepped in, carrying a tray of food, he glared at her. "You got five minutes to get to the bathroom."

She immediately hopped to her feet and walked out. As she walked past him, he grabbed her arm forcefully. "I don't need to tell you what will happen if you blow this."

"No, you don't." As she walked out, she couldn't help

but look around, but it was still the same empty hallway and the same bathroom with no working door. She sat down and quickly relieved herself. By the time she'd washed her hands, Bingo stood in the doorway, glaring at her.

As she walked back to her designated room, he muttered, "You took your sweet time."

"No," she disagreed, yet her tone was soft, quiet, and compliant. "I just had to go to the bathroom. Then I had to wash my hands and face."

He shrugged. "I don't give a shit if you wash or not, as long as you stay away from me," he muttered with a half laugh. "I don't even know why we're keeping you alive. Leverage works the same, you know, even if you're dead."

"Not true. There's a good chance Langdon will ask for proof of life."

"I can do a recording, so that's easy enough. I can even do a recording of you, screaming and begging for your life," he added, giving her a wolfish smile. She stared at him, trying for bravado but failed miserably, and he laughed. "Go sit down." Bingo pushed her into the room. "Eat. I'll be back in a few minutes to take it away."

Knowing that he would come back, and probably even sooner than a few minutes just to be an ass, she knew she had no recourse but to eat. She quickly sat down to what looked like beef stew, and no matter how she wished it, there was no water to drink. She stared at her food, swallowed hard, and proceeded to eat. She had to keep up her energy, and it's not as if she had a choice. After all, beggars couldn't be choosers, and, in her case, it didn't even matter if she begged or not. She knew that nothing would be forthcoming to make her life easier at this point.

When Bingo returned a few minutes later, he brought

her a bottle of water. "You won't get another bathroom trip anytime soon," he muttered, "so I suggest you don't guzzle it."

"Or you could lock the hallway door," she pleaded, "and leave me the bathroom. Then you don't have to come back and forth."

He snorted. "Think you're smart, don't you?"

"I'm just … Obviously this isn't what you want to do, and I don't blame you. Babysitting is never fun. … I'm just trying to make your job easier. There's only one other doorway, and you could lock it quite easily. I can't get out either way. I can just go to the bathroom by myself, which would save you some trouble."

He pondered it for a moment. "Maybe. … It would be a hell of a lot easier than coming back and forth, looking after your bladder. I've got my own to look after." Bingo then laughed uproariously.

She winced at his obvious reference to the fact that he was much more important than she was and just continued to stare at him. "It just makes sense," she repeated.

He shrugged. "I'll think about it." And, with that, he left and closed the door, locking it again.

She sighed, as she took a little sip of water. She wanted the bottle to last, but the minute you tell your mind that you shouldn't have any more, … all you can think about is more, more, and more, which would get her in deep trouble if she couldn't get out of here to the bathroom soon enough.

To have no more bathroom visits meant she would have to pick a corner of the room where she could pee, and that would just piss off Bingo even more, yet what were her options? She groaned as she immediately sent out waves to Langdon, hoping he would listen. No matter how hard she tried, there was nothing, absolutely nothing.

It seemed that her waves crashed back against her. She had no idea how to get through this building, around it, or above it. It was incredibly frustrating to have an ability that would work a lot of the time, only to have it backfire with waves of panic when you really needed it. No matter what, she had to sit here and not work her gift at all.

With that, and knowing she really needed to rest for whatever was to come, she closed her eyes, curled up into a tight ball, and went to sleep.

LANGDON MADE SEVERAL attempts to contact every person in his old team, but, so far, all that had come back was a bunch of nothing.

How are you doing?

Not sure what you're talking about.

No, heavens no.

Nah, haven't had any issues.

Some asked for more details, others were short and curt, and others didn't get back to him at all, but, so far, the messages had one thing in common, no information. There appeared to be nothing. As Langdon frowned in frustration, looking down at the list where he had just crossed off the last name, he couldn't even begin to think of another avenue to search.

He got up and hobbled around the room, swearing in frustration at his lack of movement, knowing he should be out there hunting down whoever the hell had taken Molly. Yet he had no idea where to start because he didn't know who had taken her or why. Worst case, it wasn't connected to anybody, and she had just appealed to some asshole who decided to snag her for his own purposes. That thought just about drove him mad. He was going out of his mind, and all he could do was speculate.

When his phone rang, he snatched it up and barked into it. "What?" When no response came for a second, he snapped, "What do you want?"

More silence came from the other end, and then a man with a mild tone replied, "I see life hasn't improved your temper."

Langdon winced at that. "Not sure who this is," he stated, looking at his phone. Only seeing Private Number, he cursed under his breath. "I'm really not in the mood for games."

"Of course not," the man declared, with an almost threatening tone. "I'm hurt that you don't even recognize my voice."

At that, getting an inkling of something, Langdon asked again, "Who is this?"

"Really? Even now you don't recognize it?" asked the mocking man.

Something was definitely memorable about the voice but … "Your voice is different."

There was an ugly silence on the other end. "Yeah? So maybe you do know who I am," he stated, his tone darkening. "It is different, but then you were there when it went to hell and back. Severe smoke inhalation will do that to you."

At that, Langdon sat back down as the tumblers went round and finally clicked. "Arthur?" he asked in surprise.

"Yeah, that's me," he confirmed. "Thought you'd never hear from me again, *huh*?"

"I've had no reason to think one way or the other,"

Langdon noted cautiously. "What's up?"

Arthur gave a harsh, bitter laugh. "Not a hell of a lot in my world. Though I imagine, in your world, things aren't exactly all that peachy keen."

"Why do you think that?" Langdon asked, with a darkening awareness. "What the hell is going on here, and why are you calling me?"

"I'm calling you because I have a friend of yours here."

"You have what?" Langdon asked.

"Yeah, now you're getting the message. Let's not prolong your suffering. I have Molly, your little sweet Molly. I remember listening to you talk about her all the time and how she was just the sweetest thing."

At that, Langdon stared down at his phone in horror. "If you touched a hair on her head …" he threatened, but was at a loss for words.

"Yeah? What will you do about it?" Arthur asked in a snide tone. "Last I heard, you were pretty-well laid up from surgeries, still trying to get a leg back that gives you something to walk on. You're nothing but a broken-down cripple."

"If that's all I am," he replied stiffly, taking a moment to collect himself for the hard part, "what the hell are you even doing calling me, and what do you want with Molly?" He was desperate to regain a sense of control, as he frantically sent Terk a message about this phone call. A weird sensation came in his brain, but Langdon was too focused on the phone call. "Why would you grab Molly? She's done nothing to you."

"Doesn't matter if she has or not. She's a means to an end."

Langdon stopped because that just made his blood run

cold. This man was very different from anyone else Langdon had come to know throughout his life. Arthur was always asking Langdon to help with his crimes, but Langdon hadn't heard from him recently. Arthur was a breed of his own, a sociopath with no feelings. He had no remorse, not a care for what happened to anybody else. "Why did you pick her up?" he asked. "Better yet, what do you want with her?"

"We'll talk about what I want in a minute," Arthur noted, a dark humor in his tone. "The thing is, she wants out of here, and I am sure she would like to never see me again," he added, with laughter in his voice.

"Why is that?" Langdon's voice was tight, as he gripped the phone in a clenched fist, trying to still the panic rising within him.

"Because she's not very comfortable. … Not much comfort here. She does get to go to the bathroom, or at least once or twice every twenty-four hours. I could make that happen, or I could also take it away, but it really won't be pleasant for any of us if we end up dealing with puddles in the corner, so there's that. I haven't really thought about it much to tell the truth, though it seems important to her," he muttered.

"Really? You can't be that much of an asshole," Langdon replied, trying hard to play it cool. "I told you that she has done nothing, so it doesn't make any sense at all that you picked her up. So why?"

"We did pick her up, and it does make sense. Perfect sense. You just haven't heard the whole story because, once again, you're jumping in, trying to take control and telling me exactly what I should and shouldn't be doing."

At that, Langdon snapped his jaw shut because, so far, Arthur hadn't revealed anything, but it was also very typical of Arthur to jump in and to make people sound way worse than they were. "So talk," Langdon snapped.

"*Ooh*, I just love that hospitality, that sense of … you know, 'If you don't do what I tell you, I'll reach through that phone and give you a kick in the teeth.'" Arthur spoke pleasantly enough, but a dark cloud remained there.

Langdon had to restrain himself from retorting.

"Too bad you don't have a leg to kick me. I'll call back in a little bit, when you're more amiable to what I might have to say." With that threat hanging in the air, a hard *click* came on the phone.

Immediately Terk was inside Langdon's brain. *Who was that? How do you know him? Why would he have taken Molly?*

"I used to work with him. He's an asshole, who I can't stand, and I really don't have a clue what he thinks he's doing."

He obviously has an agenda, and he seems to think that pulling Molly into it will help him get whatever he wants, Terk suggested, his voice softer. *The question is, will it? What is it that he could possibly want from you?*

"I have no idea," Langdon admitted, as he slumped back into his chair, his mind racing. "I haven't seen him in years, several years," he noted. "I can't imagine what's gone on in his world since then."

Give me his full name and details, anything that you can think of. Let me do a complete workup on him, Terk offered. *We won't understand this until we get to know our enemy.*

"Yet he's got her, Terk. He didn't ask for anything, and he will call back," Langdon shared, with a note of desperation. "I don't understand the purpose behind it and why he is toying with me."

From the conversation, I gather he's a sociopath. I imagine he's doing this to make you a little more responsive when he calls back. So, when he does come hit you with whatever it is he wants out of this, you'll be ready to work it out.

"Right," Langdon agreed. "So it doesn't matter what I want or what she wants. It's all about what Arthur wants."

It always is, Terk declared, an age-old weariness in his tone. *It always is. Send me what you can remember about this guy, and I'll get back to you, once we get a workup done.* And, with that, Terk was gone.

Langdon snatched a piece of paper and started writing down everything he knew about Arthur. They were about the same age, within about eighteen months. Langdon thought back hard and remembered his last name was Kruber, and he worked for the British government. As Langdon was going into espionage, Arthur had gone into SEAL training. He'd always wanted to be the biggest, the baddest, and the best. In many ways, he could do that without even trying. Arthur had one of those skill sets that had him rise as a leader.

Langdon wasn't even sure what happened in the meantime, but he'd lost track of the guy. He wrote down all the history he knew about him, every detail that came to him. Given that it wasn't very much, he was pretty sure Terk would get a whole lot more without Langdon's minuscule efforts. What Langdon really needed to focus on was getting off this damn leg and finding a way to get around his own insecurities and disabilities, so he could hunt her down with his gift. The question was, where to start and how.

With that, he came up with Arthur's last-known residence, then remembered a couple friends in common. It took four phone calls before he connected with somebody who was one of those mutual friends.

"Man, I haven't heard from Arthur in forever," Ned replied. "For that matter, I haven't really talked to you either. What's going on?"

Langdon hesitated, but then thought it better to be honest. "He has kidnapped my girlfriend," he admitted. "I'm trying to find any possible locations where he might have stashed her."

"Good God," Ned muttered, clearly shocked. "I hope you've contacted the police."

At that, Langdon winced. "More or less … but remember. I was in the deep end of it and doing a lot of government work. I'm not sure that would be wise at this point."

"You think Arthur is after something from your government? Maybe some information? You did some good work with them."

"It's possible, but I don't even know the latest. I'm off on medical leave at the moment because I just had a couple surgeries on my leg."

"Oh, dude, I'm sorry about that," he replied. "I really don't know what to say about Arthur. I know his family owned a warehouse just outside of Bath. However, as far I can remember, it was crumbling to pieces. I don't know if they ever sold it or not. But other than that—"

"What about the family? Do you know of any family he has?"

"No, I don't know that. There were some, but I don't know what happened to any of them."

With that little bit of information, Langdon signed off, frowning, as he stared at his notes. Something about a place in Bath. Yet finding the information would take a little bit more time.

Just then his phone rang, and he looked down to see a

number he didn't recognize. "Hello," he answered cautious-ly.

"My name is Cara," said the woman on the other end in a crisp tone of voice. "You need help with that leg, so we can find Molly. So listen. I'll work on it from here, but I need you to stop resisting."

He frowned at the phone in astonishment. "Say what?"

"I don't have time for that shit either," she declared, her tone brisk. "I need you to close out, stop thinking about anything, settle back, and just focus on your leg, so I can get to work with that." She hung up abruptly.

He shook his head, as he stared down at the phone and whistled. "Good God," he muttered. "Times have certainly changed." A laugh then came in his head, and Langdon frowned at that too. "Is that you, Terk?"

Yeah, and Cara is here too of course, he noted calmly. *The best thing you can do is listen to her and see if there's anything she can do for your leg.*

"Do you think she can?" he asked hopefully.

Sit back, relax, and we'll see. In the meantime, focus on Molly and where she might be, what kind of place she might be stashed in. Maybe she is sending you messages, so open that damn door.

He glared into the physical wall next to him, representa-tive of the mental wall in his brain, thankful they wouldn't even see that. When Cara's voice in his head came, it was clear as a whip.

I can see it just fine. Stop wasting energy.

And, with that, Langdon felt almost a mental kick that made him jolt in place and then relax. He settled back cautiously, not sure just what was happening. However, if they could do something—anything—for his leg, he would be a fool not to let them help, … as long as it helped, which was always one of his things. Due to some of the post-op problems he'd had, he worried if it would help or would hurt or would just set him back even further.

Terk's calm voice came through this time.

It will help, he confirmed, *and Cara will do as much as she can do right now. What will happen after that might be a completely different story*, Terk murmured. *Now, please, just let her work.*

With that, and not really having any other choice, Langdon settled back and focused on Molly. In his mind, he tried sending her a message. *I'm coming, sweetheart. I'm coming.*

Immediately a sense of heat came down from the top of his head and, at the same time, was pulling up from his feet. He shifted uneasily, when words, cross and exacting, came through.

Stop. He froze, and then Cara added in a much calmer tone, *Don't move.*

He didn't know how to *not* move, and it was hard, but he kept sending out signals to Molly as well. For now, it was all he could do.

CHAPTER 4

SOMEBODY GRABBED MOLLY'S shoulder and roughly jerked her to her feet. She cried out in shock and pain at the sudden shift from sleep to horrified awareness, but her captor just sneered.

"Stop sniveling," Bingo muttered. "I didn't hurt you."

Molly glared at him, then jerked her shoulder away from him. "You just like to hurt people," she muttered.

He gave her a snarky smile and nudged her forward. "The boss wants to talk to you."

She stumbled forward, not sure what Arthur could possibly want to say to her, but she figured it wouldn't be good. She didn't even have a chance to worry because she was already there.

Arthur looked at her in disgust. "Jesus, you look like shit."

She frowned at him. "I have nothing to wash with. I have nothing to sleep on but a dirt floor. You haven't even given me so much as a blanket," she stated bitterly. "So what do you expect?"

He frowned at the only other man here. "Seriously, Bingo? Not even a blanket? She does have a point."

At that, Bingo glared at Arthur. "What do you expect me to do? Produce that crap out of nowhere?"

"The least you could do is come up with a blanket for

the cold and a scrap of cardboard or something to lie on," Arthur noted in mock disgust. "We're not animals after all." He looked over at Molly. "Sorry, we didn't really think that part through." She didn't say anything and just stared at him, as he smiled. "We're really not that harsh."

It was painfully obvious that they were exactly that. If not, they wouldn't have kidnapped her in the first place.

Arthur shrugged. "Moving on." He took a breath and clarified, "And, yes, we'll try and get you a few extras to accommodate an extended stay here," he added with a half smile. "I'm certain you'll love us by the end of it all."

It was all she could do to hold back her shudder, and she knew that they were smirking at her response as it was. She didn't dare say anything, didn't dare show any more of a reaction than she already had.

Suddenly staring her down, Arthur continued. "Besides, … I need you to send a message to Langdon."

She swallowed. "What kind of message?"

"Just tell him what it is that we want and that you would like to get out of here," Arthur replied pleasantly. "All the good stuff, you know?"

"That's easy enough," she said, "because I do want to get out of here."

"Of course you do," Arthur agreed. "So I've got my phone ready to take a video. Then I'll send it to him as soon as you're done. If you're lucky, … you might even get out of here today."

No matter how simple he made it sound, she knew no way that was happening. She wasn't that lucky. Also they wouldn't have expected it to be that easy or they wouldn't have gone to the lengths they had to in order to kidnap her. "What do you want me to say?" she asked cautiously.

"Tell him that you're alive, that you're well, and that you would like to come home," he replied. "This is just a proof of life exercise. Now, anytime you feel ready."

She swallowed, then looking into the phone in his hand, she started talking. "Langdon, I'm alive. I'm well, and, yes, I would very much like to come home." Then she gave a wild laugh. "Like, I really want to come home."

At that, Arthur stopped the video, then faced her. "How very touching. I believe that'll be enough."

She just nodded because what else could she say? Short of taking a beating—which hadn't occurred, but was always implied—at five foot four and 118 pounds on a good day, a beating would break down anything she had left but her spirit. Even at that, with enough beatings, as much as she hated to think of it, her spirit would go as well. She always admired people who could be so firm and adamant that they could withstand torture. However, the reality was, the minute the beatings, the pain, and the shock of the trauma hit, most people would do absolutely anything they could to make it stop, and she knew she wasn't any different.

Suddenly she was jerked roughly to her feet again, and the boss man barked at her.

"Now you can go back and sleep again."

"With a blanket?" she asked hopefully.

He sighed. "You are nothing if not persistent," he noted, but his tone was mild, as if he were willing to give her a reward for cooperating. He looked over at her guard and stated, "Bingo, go ahead and get her something to make things a little easier on her."

Bingo just shrugged as he walked out, pushing her in front of him, muttering, "What's the point?"

She realized what he meant, and her blood ran cold. She

took his comment to mean that she wouldn't likely survive long enough to enjoy even a blanket. At that thought, her bottom lip trembled. She bit down hard, tasting blood, but what else was she supposed to do when she knew that any kind of resistance would result in a far worse consequence?

Not to mention the fact that whatever they had planned would be way worse for Langdon. Worse yet, it would be hell considering the condition he was in, … broken in body and spirit. He was so lost he could barely walk, and, with very little tolerance for self-pity, giving assistance to anyone else was simply out of the question. Yet that would be his battle. Her battle was to stay strong until somebody came and got her; assuming anybody was even looking.

In her room, she sank onto the floor and waited, hoping Bingo would come back with a blanket, but he didn't. He had basically sneered at her, as if she were too good for such things, and walked out, so it wasn't a surprise. Still, it was a disappointment. She dropped her head onto her knees, knowing that the cold would set in pretty quickly and that it would be all she could do to just stay warm.

As far as Arthur was concerned, she was living on borrowed time anyway. If there was a way to get out of this, it was with cooperation with her captors. Yet there had to be something she could do. She looked around at her space and then closed her eyes, so to anybody looking in through the little window in the door, it would appear as if maybe she was just resting, but instead she opened up her senses. Then, starting from where she was, she searched the room, poking into any and all nooks and crannies where she could slip her energy through. It was a trick she had never tried before, but, in desperate times, one must step up and try anything.

Right now this situation felt like trying anything was

required, especially if she were to survive. As she searched, going from one crack in the floor to the next, she wiggled her energy, looking for any opening to move her energy through. She kept trying, but, as she got closer and closer to the door, she still hadn't found anything. There was a space under the door, and, if she could get her energy flat enough, she could possibly sneak under it, which would get her out into the hallway.

That was something, if she could pull it off. Surprisingly enough, the trick worked. Feeling a certain amount of peace with that accomplishment, she opened her consciousness on the other side of the door and studied the hallway. She could see it, but it was like a gray space. There was no color, nothing around but a space that was increasingly gray. She felt so unmoored, with the gray walls, gray floor, gray ceiling, that it was hard to discern what was in each area. But the fact that she'd already been there before helped a lot to sort out a direction to go.

By the time she made her way down the hallway to the next door, she'd passed by the one, hesitated, then went back and snuck in underneath, struggling to change her view, so she might see something in the darkness. She waited for a long moment in the silence; the room seemed to be empty.

Except when using her vision in this form, some weird glowing things appeared. That made no sense either, but tucking away that information in the back of her brain, she headed back out the doorway and down toward the locked door she knew was at the end of the hallway. Again she struggled to see it, but, as long as she knew it was there, she would head toward it. If that would do her any good remained to be seen, not knowing what she would do when she got there. Still, as she searched forward, she thought she heard a sound. She stopped, then tilted her head, and, sure enough, heard a conversation going on around her.

"What if he doesn't do it?"

She immediately recognized Bingo's voice, complaining. There was a grumble on the other end, but it was indecisive. She waited with her breath held, even though they wouldn't know anyway. It was so bizarre that she was inside her room, yet outside of it. She hadn't done any of this kind of walking before, yet it was certainly helpful, or it could be helpful in the right circumstances. She had yet to figure out how it could help her escape though.

When Bingo grumbled again, she heard Arthur's voice.

"Stop whining."

She figured the curtness to it would make Bingo shut up immediately, but it didn't.

Bingo immediately growled. "Don't talk to me like that. I'm not your damn prisoner."

At that, Arthur laughed. "Nope, you sure aren't. As I told you, we're partners."

"Partners don't talk like that."

"Sorry," Arthur replied, with a mock exaggeration that had zero sincerity behind it.

She wondered if her hapless guard knew that Arthur was mocking him.

"That doesn't change the fact that you didn't answer my question, Arthur. ... What if he doesn't do it?"

The way he paused between statements emphasized that he was truly frustrated.

"In that case we'll find another way to get it," Arthur replied calmly.

"I'm not here just for revenge. You told me this guy we're after has big money."

"Yep, … he does. It's like Fort Knox in that place, except Langdon has abilities that can get us in there."

"What kind of abilities?"

"Based on rumors, … and stuff that I've heard, both confirm he can do it, but I don't know that he's aware that I know." Arthur laughed. "It's as if he can see ahead, as people do things. So all we need is for somebody to go in and to confirm it's there. Then we can set a charge on the safe, open it up ourselves, and get out of there."

At that, Bingo spoke again, his voice doubtful. "That's all you've got?"

"That's all I need," Arthur snapped. "I told you about this beforehand, and you said you were in."

"Yeah, I know I did," Bingo admitted, "but it's looking a little different now."

"Why? Because now you could go away for kidnapping?" Arthur asked, with a laugh. "Did you really think we would get out of this with any less than that?"

"Yeah, but she didn't even do anything."

"No, she didn't, and I can't quite believe what I'm hearing. I thought you were tired of her bickering, but, no, you're feeling sympathy for her. Bingo, that is so not you."

"That's bullshit. I just want this over with, so I don't have to deal with her."

"Right, sure." Arthur laughed. "Maybe you're starting to fancy her a little bit, *eh*?"

If she'd had blood in her veins at that moment in time, she definitely would have felt them ice over. As it was, she felt her energy shrinking back in horror, as she struggled to fight the absolute panic. Then, all of a sudden, it was too late. His words, her panic, and the energy snapped like an elastic band that had been stretched too far. Her energy slammed back into her body, and she sat, curled up in a ball, shivering.

Time to sort out what she'd accomplished. Whatever, it had worked better than she had expected, and she desperately wanted to jump up and try again. However, as she got up to try and stretch her legs, she collapsed back down again, realizing that the energy search had created a weakness, a fault within her that was dangerous.

She frowned because it shouldn't be like that. Energy should flow, easily and gently. At least that was her understanding, but maybe she had pushed it too far, too fast, or something. She didn't know, but at the moment she was not only chilled, she was seriously cold.

She carefully got up again, then walked around the room, holding onto the wall for support, as she tried to get some semblance of blood running through her veins again. Yet she shivered more and more. Finally she sat back down in her corner and curled up as tightly as she could, trying to conserve her energy and her bodily heat. She didn't understand what had happened. She certainly hadn't expected that kind of a reaction, but she would do anything for a blanket right now.

She finally dropped her head onto her arms and fell asleep. When she woke up the next time, she lifted her head, bleary-eyed, then stared around at the room for a moment, only to drop her head onto her arms once again, realizing nothing had changed.

Then came a strangled cry close to her, before she was jerked to her feet roughly, a man telling her to get moving.

"Come on. Get some blood going. What are you doing?" The tone was harsh, angry, and frustrated.

She realized it was likely Bingo again.

She whispered a mumbled word that she couldn't even recognize herself, as he kept forcing her feet forward and trying to move her arms around, flapping them like she was some sort of a bird stuck on the ground. Finally he moved her to the other room, where conversation buzzed around her, but she was disconnected from it all, involved in her own unique chatter, and she sank onto the ground, too weak to move.

She heard Arthur in the background, yelling at Bingo, then at her. "Why is she so cold?"

She was quickly wrapped up in a blanket, then picked up and put on a chair, or maybe it was a couch. She didn't care one bit which and just curled up into the actual blanket, as if it were a lifesaver, which, in her case right now, could very well be. She couldn't remember the last time she was this cold. Her teeth were still chattering, her shoulders shaking, as her body desperately tried to bring her temperature back up. Almost on cue, a second blanket was thrown across her, and then a hot drink was put into her hands, but they were trembling so badly that she spilled it all over the blanket.

With the men arguing and yelling at each other, obviously unsure what to do, she dropped her head to her knees again and closed her eyes. She didn't know how long she stayed in that stupor, but eventually she started to pull back out of it, lifting her head to look around. She noted she was still under several layers of blankets, and a heater blew directly on her as well.

She stared around the room, her gaze only half cognizant, when Arthur got up and took a closer look at her, flashing a smile.

"You're alive," he declared, with a wry note of humor in

his voice. She stared at him, unblinking. He squatted down in front of her and said, "You look a bit like an owl."

She whispered, "What happened?"

"Apparently you got very cold," Arthur stated. "I did tell that idiot to make sure you had a blanket, but he didn't listen." She just stared at him and nodded slowly. "Are you feeling any better?"

"You could have just let me die," she muttered.

He frowned. "I wasn't planning on killing you, you know."

She glared at him. "I'm not sure you planned that far ahead."

He shrugged. "Believe me. Bingo thought it was a good time for you to just not survive because then we didn't have to worry about you. But me? I felt that was hardly fair, considering you didn't have anything to do with this."

"No, I didn't," she agreed, knowing full well Arthur was lying, "so you could just let me go."

"That's not happening," he stated in a jovial tone, "but maybe now you'll be grateful to me for keeping you alive."

"How does that work? I know that you'll just try to kill me again, and, when I get that deep again, you'll probably just bring me back for kicks."

He stopped and stared at her. "I'm not a sadist."

She just stared at him, not even sure what to say to that because what kind of a man would kidnap her and hold her hostage in an attempt to get somebody else to do something? Something to do with money, at least as far as she could figure, and here she was brought back from the brink of death just to suit their plan.

He shrugged, as she continued to stare at him. "I can see that you're not convinced, and I guess that's my fault too," he admitted, with a sudden boyishness. "Sorry about that, but we'll try to do better."

She didn't say anything because *do better* didn't necessarily mean they would treat her any better, just that they would *do better to kill her* or whatever Arthur meant. She just huddled under the blankets.

Arthur looked at her in concern. "You really didn't get it, when I mentioned that you needed to get up off the ground," he replied easily. "But we've got a bunch of blankets in your room now, and, as long as you live, you can go back to your room."

She took that to mean that she was supposed to get up and move, but she wasn't at all sure. She had no idea if her legs would handle it. Still, she tried, slowly getting up, using the chair arms for support. She stumbled several steps, righted herself, and then slowly made her way toward the bathroom. She stopped, where she used the facilities, drank several small cups of water, before making her way back to the room. The doors were open, as if that would let some heat in, and maybe it would.

What did she know? She had been too cold to think straight, and even now she was on the edge of starting to shiver again. She made her way back into the room, found a bunch of blankets on the floor, and quickly curled up in them and closed her eyes yet again.

LANGDON COULDN'T DESCRIBE the feeling coursing through him right now, but it was something between pain and pleasure. It just felt so odd to have somebody working on him at this level. To think that people were even available who could do this was beyond anything he could comprehend. Where the hell were they when he had needed them last time? The voice in his head spoke with a gentle smile.

We can't be everywhere all at once.

"No, of course not," he muttered. "I'm not trying to sound ungrateful."

But it's hard not to be.

"No, that's not what I mean at all. It's been a shitty couple months, and now this with Molly …"

I get it, Cara replied. *I'm just about done with what I can do for the moment anyway. You will find that you're weak instead of energized for a couple hours. You'll need to conserve your energy to keep this healing moving forward. I'll come back in a bit.* And, with that, she was gone.

His body buzzed with this weird energy, feeling almost like somebody had an electrical machine running in the background. It was a very strange sensation, and he wasn't sure what he was supposed to do with it but figured, as long as he followed her instructions and didn't move around too much, he would be good.

God knows Langdon had plenty of healing that needed to be done. That last surgery? … He could swear the guy had messed him up more than helped him.

At that, Terk called him on the phone. "She has done all she can for the moment," he stated briskly. "She meant it when she told you to preserve all the energy you have, and that's why I'm not contacting you telepathically, since that burns through energy as well. You need to heed her warning."

"Okay," Langdon replied. "Any news on Molly?"

"No, not yet, but I've done a rundown on Arthur. It seems that he became a mercenary. His record has been clean until about four years ago. Then he got into further trouble here a couple years back and again with more trouble about two months ago. By the looks of it, he could be looking for a big score to go underground, or else he doesn't give a crap."

"What does he want with me though?" Langdon asked.

"I don't know. So the question is, what can you offer him that he can't get himself?"

"My abilities," Langdon replied, "or at least he will think that."

"Does he know about them?" Terk asked curiously.

"I'm not certain about that," Langdon replied slowly. "There was a period where we had to close the mouths busily talking. I was part of a spec program that the government was doing, almost similar to the old CIA operatives in the Cold War. The operation was set up mostly because somebody thought that I had some skills and made an attempt to get me to prove it. I wasn't into being part of a pony show," he noted. "However, I had to go through some testing, and, at that point in time, a lot of people may have found out about me. Even an article was published, which was quickly squashed."

"Sounds as if it got out," Terk noted. "You always have to worry about that type of thing."

"Exactly," Langdon muttered. "And honestly, if Arthur is looking for abilities, he'll wind up sadly disappointed."

First came silence, and then Terk asked cautiously, as if he knew already. "Why?"

Langdon sighed, then shrugged. "I told you. I've lost them."

"And as I mentioned before, my team went through a similar event," Terk reminded Langdon, "and you might find that yours will come back."

"Maybe," Langdon muttered, "but no sign of it yet."

"I can also ask Clary—Cara's twin who is also an energy healer—to have a look at that aspect. She might find something."

"If she finds anything, I would like to know myself," he declared instantly. He hesitated, then added meekly, "Does she have a solid track record with this stuff?"

"She and her sister have done some amazing work," Terk declared, his voice warm. "Their skills are quite amazing."

"God knows I could really use some help," Langdon admitted, looking down at his stump. "I also need a decent prosthetic that won't sore up the stump quite so bad."

"You probably haven't had enough time and distance from the surgery itself to be manhandling it the way you've been doing. I'm sure you are aware of that."

"Gee, look at that? It's almost as if you know me." Then Langdon laughed. "Dear God, Terk, please help me find Molly. I feel shitty enough with the way I've acted. Then I went and closed that damn door on my side too and locked it tight, leaving her stuck on her side, … and, now that she's in trouble, I can't even reach her."

"I understand," Terk noted. "It's just all too much, so maybe take on one thing at a time, okay? Molly is first."

"Glad to hear it."

"And tell me just what your abilities are."

"I can tell you what they *used* to be," he muttered. "I navigate, like, if we were coming to a crossroad, … I would know if we needed to go to left or right, depending on what it was that we were doing, and that's not a hell of a lot of help, unless you're hunting somebody. Sometimes I can see what a person does before they do it, but that's iffy."

"It's a huge help in many cases. Can you pull back out of

the picture and look at a map and decide left or right as well?"

"Yes, in a general way. If we were hunting, … say, we're in Iran, and we were looking for somebody, and we had a city, maybe a huge place to search, I could generally … put us in the right direction. If we're looking for somebody in a house, generally I could put us or direct people to the right location."

"Interesting," Terk noted. "That's a very handy thing."

"Sure, but it's kind of a parlor trick, and right now? I don't even have that available to me."

"As I said before, it will all come back, and, in most cases, our abilities came back even stronger."

"You already had more abilities than anybody I ever knew," Langdon muttered. "The telepathy that you can operate, going into people's heads like you do, without any thought or not even knowing that person, not to mention no boundary on distance, that's just freaky."

"And yet you're perfectly capable of doing it yourself. If I can come into your head, you can come into mine."

At that, Langdon stopped. "I never thought of it that way," he mumbled cautiously. Was it that simple? He frowned, thinking of the possibilities.

"No, most people can't, but, if you have access in one pathway, you have access in them all."

"Damn." He brightened for the first time in days.

"Exactly," Terk stated.

"So, by contacting you, I'm also opening myself up to the same kind of contact, though not necessarily with the same finesse?"

"Ouch, I can just imagine the headaches," Terk admitted. "Yeah, you have no idea. Sometimes people don't know how to get in, and they stand outside and scream at me, until I'm deaf," he muttered. "Yet, at the end of the day, it's still a heck of a way to communicate."

"It's unbelievable to most," Langdon noted. "I presume that, if you could find Molly, you could communicate with her that way as well?"

"I have been searching," Terk shared, "and that's one of the reasons. I'm trying to figure out why I can't find her. It's unnerving."

"What situations would block you from connecting?"

"It depends. If she's underground in a steel-lined area of some kind, maybe that. I hate to say it, but a walk-in safe, like a bank vault, could hinder my connections. I couldn't get into that if it's deep underground, if she's super weak, or if there's any masking going on."

"Masking?" Langdon repeated.

"Yeah, if somebody else is blocking me," Terk replied. "People like to mask what they're doing, and, even if they don't know they have any skills, it's amazing how much they can do."

"I can imagine," Langdon muttered.

"Still, we have to work with the people we can help, and that is a completely different story. I've put out feelers for her energy, which I've gotten from you by the way."

At that, Langdon reared back and looked around the room. "Okay, … you want to explain that?"

"Not right now," Terk said hurriedly. "Have to go." With that, the phone went dead.

Langdon looked down at it, shaking his head. *Damn.* It was one thing to have a friend who you trusted to be in your head, but it was another thing completely to know that somebody like Terk could step in and out, and you had absolutely no say in the matter. And, of course, he knew Terk would say absolutely Langdon did have a say in the matter and could butt Terk out at any time. Still, that didn't stop people who didn't have anything to do with this industry from freaking out. Langdon had heard rumors about Terk's incredible abilities and awesome powers, but, of course, the gossip elevated them to the point of being ludicrous. Or were they?

Langdon got up, grabbing his crutches, slowly hobbled forward, expecting to have his leg throbbing within minutes, but so far, so good. He went to the bathroom and then headed to the kitchen to grab some food. Taking his meal with him, he sat down at the computer for the first time in God-only-knows how long, without the pain racking through his system.

He was afraid that Cara would jump in and tell him to stop and to lie down again, but that didn't happen. Surely, if he was sitting with his leg up, he would be okay. He quickly shifted his body to make sure he had it properly elevated. He needed to hunt down that property in Bath.

Thinking about that, he quickly sent off a message to Terk with that information again, hoping that somebody could track it down on their end too. If anybody had access, Langdon needed any advantage he could get. He got a response almost immediately.

They are on it.

And that's the thing. Everybody *was* on it.

Everybody was doing something to find her, except him. And that just made Langdon feel completely useless. How could he help? There had to be something.

CHAPTER 5

WHEN MOLLY WAS woken the next time, she managed to get to her feet a little bit better than the last time. She wasn't quite so cold, although she thought it would be days before that innate chill settled down. She was dragged to the washroom and then stepped out, only to be motioned toward the boss again. Grabbing a blanket, she followed Bingo.

As she entered the other room, Arthur eyed her critically. "That's better. It looks like you'll make it this time."

She nodded. "Thank you," she replied. "I was pretty sure I was a goner."

"I wasn't so sure about it myself," he stated, still studying her. "But you do appear to be improved, so that is a good thing."

"Yeah," she agreed. "It's amazing what a little bit of heat can do."

He laughed. "True enough." He pointed to the side. "Sit over there."

Ah, that same chair again. He directed her to sit on the one chair she'd sat on last time. Not sure why or what the point was, but she sat quietly and waited, while he brought up the phone and called somebody. A beep repeated, noting the line was busy on the other end, something Arthur surely was not expecting.

He frowned. "I'll give him a couple more chances, and then I'll send you back to your room, until I can reach him."

She nodded. "Did you ever hear back? Any response to the video?" she asked hesitantly.

"Haven't sent it yet," Arthur admitted, "but I think I will now."

She wondered why he'd held back or if he was planning to just keep it for later. No way to understand what was going on in Arthur's mind, but he definitely had an agenda, and he would play it out, no matter what she did. She could either go along with it or get out of his way. Personally, she was totally okay with getting out of his way, but she would prefer that he got out of her way too.

He tried several more times. Then, with a wave of his hand and disgust on his face, he turned to Bingo. "Take her back to her room."

She quickly got up and moved back to her room, as she heard Bingo's objection.

"What the hell is he doing?"

Arthur replied, "He's apparently busy, so what else am I supposed to do? The guy probably has no idea what's going on. It's not as if we've given him a clue."

"Why don't you send the video?" Bingo asked.

"Because I didn't want to. Not yet. I was hoping he would go along with the plan without me forcing the issue. But, as it is, I'm sending it now." He walked over to his laptop and sat down.

She heard him clicking away on the keyboard. Then their voices dropped, and she couldn't hear anymore. She closed her eyes and reached out once again to Langdon, asking him to please pick up. *Come on. Hear me. Listen to me. If ever I needed you, I need you now.* But got no answer.

She returned to her room on her own, fell asleep right away, mostly because of the cold building up again in her body. She was sure that she had exhausted herself. When she woke up again, instead of being brought to the other room, she woke to find Arthur standing in the doorway, leaning against the door frame, a camera in his hand.

"I gather you sent it then," she said.

He nodded, as he kept filming.

She huddled against the blanket, hating that sense of invasiveness, as he kept coming closer. She wouldn't play his game, whatever it was. By the time he had whatever length of video he wanted, he turned and headed back out again. She got to her feet, then slowly made her way to the bathroom, grateful they had left the door open for her to do that much, and then she noted the door beside them was open as well.

However, that room was empty. It had been empty when she'd seen it last, and, as she crept forward, until she could look inside, it was still empty. The odd thing was, it seemed warmer than her room. She frowned, wondering if she dared stay in here because a heater was in that room. That must have been the glowing she had seen earlier. As she stood here, staring at it, the other door opened, and her guard stepped out, glaring at her.

"Wow," Bingo said, openly snickering, "looks like you're ready to get a good smacking."

She stared at him. "I was hoping I could move into this room. A heater is in there," she explained in a low voice. "I'm … I'm still cold."

He frowned, then looked at the room, but it was obvious that he could figure it out himself.

She quickly added, "I didn't open this door. … It was already open."

"I know it was," he replied, then pondering her request, he shrugged. "I guess no reason not to."

She smiled, then returned to her room and grabbed her blankets, quickly stepping into the heated room. Almost immediately she felt her senses starting to warm. "Oh, thank God," she whispered. She still was huddled on the floor, but now she was beside a heater.

Bingo laughed. "You really have it bad."

She didn't know what she was supposed to say to that. She'd been kept here underground for who-knows-how-many days, with no heat and a bare minimum of food. She was so low on sleep that, on top of the stress and duress, it only made sense that her body was sucking up all the available heat. She curled up, closed her eyes, and willed Bingo to go away.

As it was, he just stood there, staring at her, an odd look on his face that she didn't dare catch.

She pretended to ignore him, until finally he gave a snort almost in disgust and walked away, but that may have been due to hearing his buddy call him. She wasn't sure what Bingo was up to or what he planned to do, but the more he looked at her, the worse it felt.

The last thing she wanted was for him to take a personal interest in her. At this point, being ignored was way better than anything else, as far as she was concerned. Just the thought of Bingo staring at her with that weird gaze was enough to make her skin crawl. She shuffled a little deeper under the blankets and forcibly pushed away those thoughts.

GETTING UP AND walking around, Langdon slowly started

to strengthen his leg, giving a little bit of exercise to the good leg and standing for seconds at a time with the amputated leg hanging down, still waiting for that pressure to build up that would tell him to lift it up again. However, whatever Cara had done seemingly had a positive effect. It was just too bizarre, but still, Langdon was ecstatic.

He also knew that, if he did too much, it would push back the healing. So he finished printing off all the information he had found online, and, with that, he went to his couch, where he could prop up his leg again. There, he quickly sifted through the information, looking for anything that would give him an idea of where Molly was. It was a completely ugly spread, and ironic that here he was, somebody who would normally say where to go looking. Yet he couldn't get even an inkling as to where she was.

Of course he knew that was entirely because of his accident, and the only thing he could hope for was that whatever healing took place right now would be enough to help save her life.

CHAPTER 6

B ACK IN HER newly designated room, wrapped up in blankets and shivering like there was no tomorrow, even though the heater was in here, Molly wondered how long it would be before someone could get her the hell out of here. So far, she'd been given minimal food, minimal water, and limited access to the bathroom. On top of that, she was so cold. She left the door open, and nobody had come to close it.

Even as she sat here, she heard them talking, but the voices were more indistinct mumbles, as if they had no start and no finish, just this consistent buzzing in her ears. It was like being in the gray world. Her energy was still at a very low point, since she'd burned through so much of it so fast. Yet here she was, trying hard to get control all over again. As she moved out to the doorway and peered around the corner, she saw the men out there, talking furiously, but it was still hard to hear.

Why? That buzz? Or something else? She slipped a thread of energy toward the men, then slipped around them and underneath the doorway, until she found herself in a hallway.

It was a commercial-looking building, and she saw a big Exit sign at the far end. Excited, she poured more energy in that direction, but her heart was slamming against her chest.

That was the first sign that she was burning through way too much energy again. Her body trembled, but she couldn't ignore that hint of freedom, knowing that, if she might get a peek outside, maybe she could see where she was.

Maybe she could send the information to somebody. A receiver out there who was listening. She didn't know what else to do, so she kept pouring energy into the thin energy thread, as she headed toward the Exit sign. Then the most bizarre thing happened, and she had no idea how, but it was like somebody stepped right through her energy. It was the strangest sensation, as if that piece of her had been cut off, as if it came into contact with something like a massive wall or maybe a sword that cut it in two.

Feeling bereft and cut off from that energy, her focus wavered, and her energy was snapped together. She was slammed with the energy she had sent out, and it reeled all the way back to her body, back to her soul, leaving her trembling once again.

What the hell? What had just happened?

Hard footsteps thundered down the hallway to the second door, and then they stopped. Bingo, her captor, glared at her suspiciously. "Did you say something?"

She looked at him, her teeth starting to chatter again, and shook her head. "No," she whispered. "I didn't."

He frowned. "What's wrong with you now? Damn it, woman. What the hell was your family even thinking about. … They should have just deep-sixed you at birth. Way too fragile." Thinking that was a hilarious joke, he turned and left her.

She pulled the blankets over her head tent-style and burrowed into the tightest cocoon that she could, trying to warm up. His words hurt, but more than that she felt a sensation of wrongness. What had brought him to her was probably one of the two men outside were responsible for snapping her energy thread.

Was Arthur's energy so thick, so unyielding, that it could separate hers? She'd never had anything like that happen before, but then again she had never done this before either. She wanted to laugh; she wanted to cry, yet she was far too exhausted and too weak to do either. When she heard more footsteps coming down the hallway, she realized that Bingo had probably said something to Arthur, and now he was coming to gloat.

When the blanket was jerked roughly off her head, Arthur looked at her in concern, her teeth chattering yet again. She wrapped her arms around herself and snatched the blanket from his hands and bundled up again.

"Good God," he muttered. "Look. I'll go get you a coffee. Maybe that'll help." He quickly disappeared.

The coffee would help. Whether it was because of the heat or the caffeine, she didn't know, but she relished the thought of getting some anyway. By the time he returned, she was sitting up with the blankets tucked up around her neck, one hand free. She looked up expectantly at the mug, a thick, cheap porcelain mug, but she couldn't have been happier to find it full of steaming hot coffee.

She nodded her thanks.

He stared at her for a moment, still frowning, then shook his head. Without any comment, he turned and walked back out. "I don't know what's wrong with her," he announced to his partner.

The partner laughed. "She's just weak. They're all weak. Women are just like that."

"No, women aren't like that," Arthur argued. "And you

and I both know it. Just because you've been burned a few times doesn't mean you can blame all women."

"Maybe," Bingo acknowledged, "but something's wrong with this one."

Arthur asked him, "What made you get up and walk over there anyway?"

"I don't know. I thought I heard something. Then, when I got closer, I felt these cold waves. I don't know what it was, but, by the time I got down to her door, she was just huddled over and shivering."

"Yeah, she's way too cold."

"I know she's tiny, and there's no body fat on her either, but I guess we haven't given her enough food, have we?"

"She's still alive, isn't she?" Arthur snapped. "But we also need her to be cognizant and capable of responding to any kind of request. No matter what you feel, or how you flip this, we need that woman to keep Langdon in line."

"I don't know about all that. Just hold her head up in a basket and tell Langdon that he'll be next if he doesn't do what we want," Bingo stated in a harsh voice. "I didn't come here to babysit."

"Then go off and do your thing for a while," Arthur suggested. "Get out of here. Go on. It would be good for you to take some time off, but maybe bring back some food or something."

"Yeah?"

"Yeah, I mean it. Just go. Bring back some beer, some subs maybe. I don't know, … maybe some fried chicken, something hot too, … seeing as she's freezing in there."

"Yeah, and that's just wrong. It's like she's really ill."

"Maybe, but now is not the time to debate the issue. Go to the store and pick up something to help, like a sleeping bag or something."

"What do you think I'm made of, money?"

Molly heard a rustle, as if Arthur were pulling money from his pocket, and then the sound of coins and something hitting the table.

"Take that and go," Arthur ordered, "and maybe stop at the pub and have a beer or two. You are starting to grate on my nerves."

There was a scraping sound, and boots hit the floor with a rush. "Now that is a hell of a good idea, and, while I'm gone, you can deal with that goddamn video and tell your buddy what will happen. Set up a phone call and get this shit sorted out. I'm not coming back to babysit her for another week, while your buddy figures out what to do."

"I hear you, Bingo. I hear you," Arthur replied.

She heard hard footsteps as Bingo headed toward the door. When it slammed shut, she heard Arthur's snapping steps in the empty room.

She smiled because any division between the two of them was good for her. She stayed curled up, afraid that Arthur would come toward her, but instead it sounded like he was trying to dial somebody on the phone. He had it on Speakerphone, and she heard it buzzing, as if it were busy. When it didn't go through again, he swore and tossed the phone on the table, then wandered around for a bit. Finally he sat down and turned the phone back on again. This time he snapped, "Where the hell is he?" He tossed the phone again. A moment later, Arthur muttered something about time and something else indistinct.

Molly wished she could get back out there with her energy and try to look for more clues as to what was going on. Surely only Bingo had noticed her energy or that cold wave, though it shouldn't be cold, except that she was so damn cold it would cost too much of her own heat energy to keep her going if she tried to heat that too.

It made no sense. She sat here, wondering at the sanity of making another attempt at streaming her energy. What if she opened up her transmitter again and sent out signals, hoping desperately that somebody could hear her in here? It had been a faint hope that she could get up to that Exit door and send a message. At that, she sat up straighter, wondering if she could sneak even a tiny thread out to that Exit door to get underneath and outside to send messages.

Would anybody hear? Would Langdon get it?

She quickly decided it was worth the risk, even if she fell into a coma. Either she would die or it would be her captors' problem to look after her or not. Separating off one very fine thread of energy, she snaked it out of her room into the other one. She noted that Arthur was off to the right, on what appeared to be a couch. He was focused on his laptop, so she snuck under the door, heading as fast as she could to the Exit sign.

As soon as she got to the Exit, huge rubber weatherstripping reinforced the threshold, but the corner gave her just a tiny fraction of a space, and she slipped out. When she hit the fresh air, she started screaming as loud as she could to the ethers. She was desperately sending out as loud and as strong of a message as she could, hoping that somebody would hear.

Just when she thought her energy wouldn't hold, and she felt all her resources fading, she heard a tiny whisper of a voice in the back of her head.

Gotcha.

WHEN THE RINGING phone woke him up from the deep sleep he fell under, after Cara had worked on him, Langdon stared at the phone in confusion and drowsiness. "Yeah," he answered, his tone surly. He couldn't control the bitterness because honestly it was the first decent sleep he'd had in months.

"I got something for you, and I'm sending it to your phone," and, with that, Arthur hung up.

With his heart sinking and his stomach clenching in fear, Langdon clicked on the link that immediately appeared. What he saw appeared to be a short video of Molly sitting in a chair untethered but looking exhausted and scared. She looked like a ghost, obviously focused on sending a message that she was fine. He studied it nervously but saw no sign of her having been beaten or abused. When the phone rang a second time, he answered immediately. "What do you want from me?"

"If you want her back home," Arthur stated, "I'll need something from you."

"Of course you do. You never were the kind of guy to do something for nothing."

"See? That's why we should have been best friends. You knew everything there was to know about me."

"You're a psychopath who doesn't give a shit about any-thing," he muttered. "That's what I know, but apparently you know way too much about me."

"Yeah. Absolutely I do." Arthur laughed. "When you think about it, I'm doing you a favor."

"How do you figure that?" Langdon asked.

"This is setting your priorities straight, isn't it?"

At that, Langdon frowned. Just what the hell did Arthur mean by that? It was definitely an odd statement, coming from him. Had Molly mentioned something about their relationship? Surely not.

"So, let me just remind you. This little girlfriend of yours? … She's not doing all that great. The video was taken yesterday, and I have to admit she's kind of sunken a bit lower since then."

Just enough sincerity filled his tone to make Langdon sit up straighter. "What did you do to her?" he growled. "If you hurt her …"

"What? You'll come here and kick me? Oh, wait, but you won't kick me, will you?" he asked, with a laugh. "You've only got one leg. After all, if you kick me, you'll end up with your ass on the floor. So, yeah, what will you do?" he sneered. "God, it figures you would be some do-gooder who went and got your ass kicked on a job. You should have been at a desk, but there you were, out in the action, getting your ass hurt. You know, for all of five minutes, I felt sorry for you, until I remembered all the times you beat me in pool, and I realized I wasn't sorry at all. As a matter of fact, I was thinking it was kind of … *fair* in a way and oddly satisfying for me. After all, just think about it. … I was a good guy. You were the bad guy, and yet you kept kicking my butt."

"Obviously you needed a kick," Langdon muttered. "You've been preaching at me for a good five minutes, and you still haven't said what you want."

"What I want," he replied, "are the numbers to a safe."

At that, Langdon stared at the phone in shock. "You want what?"

"Yeah, the numbers to a safe. See? I heard from a little birdie that, while you were out on a mission, you somehow managed to magically get the numbers to a safe, so they could get it open and get what they wanted, and everybody got out scot-free. Except for you of course, but that's a whole different story—just because you couldn't keep your ass out of the line of fire."

"That wasn't my fault or anybody else's."

"Yeah, right, … except yours." Arthur still chuckled, but his tone turned dark. "According to them, you didn't need any help, and you could turn that lock, as if you knew the combo. The only way they figured you could do that was if you had some otherworldly skills. I heard all kinds of rumors about you having skills like that. Now that there is a life on the line, you wouldn't be holding out on me, would you?"

He stared at the phone. "You lost me at picking locks without any trouble," he snapped. "And you're still not making sense ten sentences later."

Arthur's tone got ugly. "I don't care what games you want to play because I hold the upper hand. She's here with me, whether you like it or not, and, if I don't get what I want, she just might not survive this. Honest to God, she's already shivering so much right now, I don't get it."

At that, all Langdon's alarm bells went off. "Look. She has a real problem with temperature control. She probably should be living in Florida or something. She's always cold."

"Yeah, she's cold all right," Arthur confirmed. "She can hardly even talk between her teeth chattering."

"You got to warm her up then, or she'll get hypothermic."

"I don't really care if she does or not, as long as you do what you're told. However, I won't do a damn thing, … not until I have what I need. Get me those numbers."

"Even if I got those numbers for you, no telling how you would handle it. I want her released first, before I do anything."

"That's nice, but you're not calling the shots here. This is my deal. I need what's in that safe, and, from there, we'll see. If I get away with it pretty smooth and easy, I can sure see where I might want to use those skills again."

"Which means you'll never release Molly anyway," Langdon stated, his voice harsh. "So why the hell should I have anything to do with this?"

"I could just kill her right now. That's always an option," Arthur noted. "You don't have any family left, and neither do I, so it's not as if we can sit here and play the kill-off-each-other's-family game. Thus, since that won't happen, I suggest you do it my way, and she'll get out of here alive."

"Not if you won't let her go at the end of this job," he muttered.

"I'll always find you somewhere, so I'm okay to let her go, though it is kind of tempting to think about you doing this again and again. I was even thinking that I might have to kill off my partner here because the haul wouldn't quite be big enough for me to live on forever, not without having to do this kind of work again," he muttered. "But, if you can do this, … my partner does help look after her, so it just makes sense to keep him around after all."

Langdon heard a door slamming in the background on the other end of the call. Harsh voices and then Arthur's slightly maniacal laughter.

"Oops, my partner heard that," he admitted in a silky voice. "I've got to run. Now I have some damage control to take care of." With more of the same laughter, the call was abruptly terminated.

Moments later the phone rang, and Terk's voice came through. "Are you okay?"

"No, I'm not. Arthur just called again, tormented me some more nonsense about the combination to a safe."

"Interesting request really."

"He seems to think there's some big score he can walk away with, but he did mention something about killing off his partner, so he didn't have to share the haul. But then he said, if I could do this, maybe he would hang on to Molly, so I could help him again and again."

"Of course that will be the problem, won't it? Why release Molly if he can keep you doing these jobs?"

"Exactly," Langdon muttered, and almost immediately he heard a weird buzz in his head. "Ouch, my head. Is that you, Terk?"

"Nope, not me. That's Cara. She is also asking you to stop doing this, stop the overdrive. She's coming in to work on you."

Almost immediately Langdon found himself flat on his back, and a weirdly delicious feeling moved through his body. "What the hell is that?" he cried out.

It's me, Cara snapped. *I have to do this every so many hours in order to keep up the healing flow. So shut up and let me work, so I can go back to sleep.*

He immediately shut up, wondering what was going on and who could so casually tell him off and bend him to her will, when obviously he had other plans. Who the hell was this woman?

Somebody who cares, Cara snapped, *not just about you but about humanity and definitely about Molly.*

"Yeah, Molly," Langdon muttered, closing his eyes, hating that the hot tears were never far from the surface.

Crying is not something to be ashamed of, she growled. *A lot of men would be a whole lot better off if they would just let out some of their emotions.*

"Maybe, but I've never found that it changed anything."

Maybe not, Cara obliged, *but your psyche would thank you.*

He asked her, "Do you really think it makes a difference?"

It absolutely makes a difference. You're holding all that stress inside, when you should be letting it go, releasing it to the world around you and trying to heal, instead of hanging on to all that shit.

"Right, thanks for the pep talk."

There. I'm done now for a bit, she stated, and, with that, she was gone.

Not too long afterward, he dropped into bed, fast asleep.

The next morning he slowly got up and made his way to the shower to scrub down, top to bottom. He realized that it was the first time in weeks that he had slept and that he felt this good. He knew it had to be from her energy work, and even trying to support himself in the shower was a whole lot easier today. Finally finished, he opened the glass door and grabbed the crutch that he always kept close by, then hopped out, dried off, and, with fresh clothing on, made his way out to get the coffee going.

He had barely gotten the coffee made when a knock came on the door. It opened, without him even reaching for it. He stared at Riff and Rick, as they stormed inside. A stranger was at their side.

The newcomer stepped forward and shook his hand. "I'm Eton."

Then Langdon turned to the other two, who wore big grins on their faces. "Did you find her?" Langdon cried out, looking at their expressions.

Immediately their smiles disappeared, and they shook their heads. "No," Riff admitted, "but we did get something."

"Like what?" Langdon glared at them, hating that his hopes had arisen so quickly, only to be dusted just as fast.

"We found out that she was snatched just outside of her house. She was picked up by a white van that had been stolen the previous night. The owner used the van for work and went out the next morning to find it gone. The cops found it fairly quickly afterward, parked on a side street not very far from where it was taken in London. Not realizing it had been used in a crime, they quickly signed off the paperwork and returned it. No forensics were done or anything, and the owner had been using it steadily ever since. We found the owner and spoke to him, but he didn't really want to give us his vehicle, so we ran quite a few forensic tests on it there and then. We did come away with a couple hairs and some fingerprints," Riff explained. "One was smudged, looking like there was an attempt to wipe it off, so it's only a partial of the thumb, but one of the hairs looks to be Molly's."

"We needed some way to cross-reference that, so we went to her place and did a full check there and grabbed some DNA from a hairbrush for comparison tests. We're still waiting for a check on the other hair."

"It's not the owner's?" Langdon asked, his hopes rising yet again. This roller coaster of emotions was killing him more than anything else.

"Not the owner's, correct," Rick replied. "We did take a hair sample from him for comparison. So, everything's at the lab right now, and they'll rush the tests. Including the fingerprints."

At that they both gave him fat grins. Eton was listening intently, as if trying to catch up.

Langdon stared at them, feeling like he had missed something. "I get that you guys think this is great, but I already had an ID on who it is who took her," he mentioned, bewildered. "So what does this give us?"

At that, Rick sighed and added, "Because now we've got enough to bring everybody in back home. Now they can all put their laptops to work and join in the hunt. We'll track that vehicle on the city cameras, which, in a city this size, are at every intersection."

At that, Langdon stared at them, first in shock and then in joy. "Oh my God, finally a break."

"Exactly," Rick confirmed, as he walked over and poured coffee for all of them and sat down.

As he accepted the cup, Langdon looked over at them. "I heard from Arthur too, by the way."

"Okay, and what is it that he's after?"

"Combination to a safe. A loaded one too."

At that, Rick frowned at him. "Okay, I'm confused. I understand that you can sometimes find directions but a safe?"

Langdon nodded slowly.

"So, what the hell does directions have to do with sorting out or breaking into safes?" Rick asked.

At that, Langdon looked at him, and his lips twitched. "Remember how I find those directions?"

Rick just stared at him blankly.

"Remember? Left-right, right-left ..."

Rick's eyes widened in shock. "Holy crap, that's how you find the code for the safe, isn't it? You turn to the left until it tells you to stop, and then you go back again."

He nodded. "Exactly. The tumblers are all built basically the same way. Now there are no absolutes in our world, but I have yet to find one that I couldn't open relatively easily." At that, the trio of men looked at him with additional respect.

"That's a very handy little tool," Riff noted, studying him carefully. Eton nodded in agreement. "The question is, how does this guy know you can do that? I presume you were smart enough to keep it out of the dailies."

"Ya think? I didn't know that anybody knew. I was on the job for the government, and we did have quite a FUBAR over one op. I was called in because one of the guys was hurt and couldn't get through security. It was fairly close to where I was, so I ended up jumping on board, and they couldn't get the safe open. I went down, and I opened it, … and I guess I did it easily enough that it caused suspicion."

"Crap."

"Yeah, exactly. That's not something I would want anybody to know, but apparently not only does somebody know but unfortunately the wrong kind of somebody knows."

"Yeah, you're not kidding," Rick muttered. "In this case, the wrong people are deadly."

Langdon nodded. "That's why, no matter whatever the hell is going on here, Molly needs to get out of it safely. Arthur did say that she wasn't doing so well and was always cold and shivering. She really needs to be rescued and fast."

"Does she get cold a lot?" Eton asked.

"Yes, she does but not dangerously so. She will be trying to do whatever she can to get away, while trying to hide the fact that she has abilities herself. Hers are not so defined, but she will do whatever she can to escape."

"Can she talk like we do with Terk?" Rick asked.

"We all can do that apparently," Riff added, with an eye

roll.

"No," Eton spoke up, shaking his head. "You guys can. I'm one of the normal people in this world."

"No abilities?" Langdon asked in surprise. It seemed everyone in Terk's world had abilities.

"No abilities," he confirmed. "And I do just fine without them. Still, it's nice to watch you guys as you work and to get an idea about some of these gifts you have."

Langdon switched his gaze to Riff. "When did you realize you could communicate telepathically?"

"Only with Terk," he muttered in disgust. "That man just jumps in and out of my brain and gives it a good shake while he's at it, as if I'm not listening to him, then jumps back out again."

At that, Rick started to laugh. "Terk's good at that, but it's also a very handy skill to have when we're under duress."

"Yeah, I know," Langdon agreed, "and it helps me in many ways. I just wish he could do it for Molly."

"He has a line on her energy," Rick shared, "but, if she's hidden or someplace where Terk can't reach her, then he cannot communicate. But, if she's out in public, he can search and find her signature. Then it's a whole lot easier for him. Still no guarantee, but I haven't seen him fail more than a half-dozen times."

"Right. ... I sure as hell hope she's not one of the few fails," Langdon muttered. "It's driving me crazy, knowing she's held by this lunatic. I don't know who his partner is, but Arthur was joking about shooting him for his share. The partner walked in, while Arthur was still laughing about it, and Arthur had to do some damage control, so I don't know what the hell that means."

"Let's see if we can come up with who the hell this guy is

who drove the stolen vehicle," Eton suggested.

"If it happens to be the partner, that would be good because then we could get some information on him and maybe track down everything we need to know about your friend."

"No friend of mine," Langdon corrected, with curt feelings. "Especially now."

"No, maybe not," Rick agreed, "but we have to get in his head and understand what makes him tick. In this case, the guy seems to have a lot of smarts and a lot of balls."

"He does, but I'm not sure that he cares. He's deep in the hole. He has no money and no resources. So either way it's not so much about the game as it's the end result for him. Honestly I would say he's a psychopath or sociopath, whichever one doesn't give a shit about feelings because that's him. He's cold as ice, and he's been in this world playing these games for a very long time. They're well suited to him because he really doesn't connect with people. That was my problem with him before. He just didn't care. What he wanted came first, and everything else was secondary."

"Gotcha," Riff noted. "I'll grab my laptop, then sit at your table and start tracking some of those traffic cams. I'll check in with the others to see where they are, and we'll go from there." He looked over at Rick. "Do you want me to grab yours?"

Rick nodded, as he looked back at Langdon. "I haven't slept in a while. Is it okay if I crash either on the couch or on your bed for a few hours?"

"Go for it," Langdon replied. "You guys are helping me out, so whatever I can do to help you."

At that, Riff snorted. "I'm glad to see this change of attitude." He glared at Langdon, as he stepped out the door, slamming it behind him.

"Is he always like that?" Langdon asked.

Eton grinned. "From the bit I've had to do with him, yes. But he's good at what he does. Just stay out of his way."

"Yeah, he is good, at least for the time I've known him, but that hasn't been all that long," Rick confirmed. "Riff's definitely somebody who cuts to the chase. He wasn't terribly friendly or agreeable when we first arrived, but, like him, I'm glad to see there's been a few changes. How are you doing?"

"Better, I guess. Cara has been working on my leg, doing something to help with healing it and taking the pain down to something that might be manageable," Langdon shared, with a half smile. "And it helps to know who has Molly and why, even if I don't know where she is. It does give me some answers, and now we'll make some progress. ... My apologies for being an ass when you were here earlier, but I wasn't really giving a shit about niceties."

"No, we get it," Rick replied, heading toward the bed. "Niceties aren't part of the job. It's just a whole lot easier to work with people when they know we're not working against them."

"Got it. How long will you sleep?"

"I was hoping for four, but we'll see if you need me sooner," And, with that, Rick disappeared into the bedroom.

Immediately Riff showed back up at the door and headed in, carrying two laptops. Heading straight to the table, he set up his laptop and got to work, while Eton took over Rick's laptop while he slept, leaving Langdon sitting here, wondering what he could do to help.

By the looks of it, he could just wait and do nothing. He hated that, but whatever it took.

CHAPTER 7

MOLLY FROZE, AS the voice whispered to her again.

I'm here. Don't let anybody know.

I won't, she whispered back in her head. Then she gave her head a hard shake. *Who are you?*

Terk.

Her eyebrows shot up. *How the hell did you find me?* she asked, her voice rising in a crescendo of excitement.

Immediately he whispered, *Shh.*

She winced. *Sorry, but I'm only speaking to you in my head, not out loud.*

Yeah, but you're hurting my ears, he relayed, with a note of amusement.

Pardon me for being excited, but being a captive and stuck in here all alone hasn't been the highlight of my life.

I'm sorry for that, he muttered, *but I'm here now. I'm just not sure what I can do at this point.*

How did you even find me?

I caught a whiff of your signature outside and then it kind of changed.

Oh my, she exclaimed. *I managed to get a little bit of my energy outside the Exit door and tried screaming for help.*

So, that would be what I caught, Terk noted. *I have to say that was a smart move. I came back in, following your energy, but I'm not capable of moving or seeing anything around you.*

That's what I found too. It's all grayscale out there, she noted in confusion. *I can't send any messages out from inside. I had to get outside the door to do that, and then that door closed, and I haven't been able to get back out there again.* After a moment of hesitation, a weird buzzing happened in her head.

You're not doing so well, Terk stated, his tone sharp. *Did they hurt you?*

No, but my energy is fading quickly. I don't know if it's this environment, the stress, the energy depletion, or whatever, but, whenever I try to do something, it strips me of everything I have to give, and then I'm in trouble. I get terribly shaky and super cold.

Interesting, he murmured. *It could be the environment. I didn't have a chance to see anything, so I don't know where you are.*

Me neither, she muttered, *but the fact that you even found me is massive.* She could sense rather than see his smile. Her own spirits rose. She was no longer alone.

It's definitely progress, but we have to get past this right now, he stated. *Do you know anything about it?*

I just know the one guy's name is Arthur. The other is Bingo.

Yeah, we know that too. He has approached Langdon for help, … something about breaking into a safe.

She pondered that. *I don't understand how Langdon could do that and why this guy cares.*

I think there's some drug dealing going on or something, and Arthur wants whatever is in the safe. He's referring to the contents as money, but I'm not sure that is true. We never really trust anything that comes from these guys.

No, she agreed, her energy thin and shaky. *I'm so glad*

you found me, she mumbled, barely holding back the tears. *Thank you.*

You're welcome, and just know that we're working on finding you physically, Terk reminded her. *Stay strong and know that we'll be around.* Just then came an odd shift in the background. *I hate to say it, but I have to go.* And, with that, Terk was gone.

Her energy snapped back, jolting her. She sat here, a smile on her face, realizing that, for the first time in a very long time, she wasn't all alone. Terk had found her. That provided her with a sense of freedom and relief that was almost impossible to hold back. Yet she would have to remember not to wear that smile in front of her captors.

She heard voices raised in the other room but wasn't sure what was going on. However, it didn't sound good. While she was more than delighted to have a fight happening between them because she thought that might strengthen her position to get out of here, still that guy Bingo scared the crap out of her.

Arthur, on the other hand, scared her in a completely different way, but this Bingo, her captor and the one who had been guarding her the whole time? Something was very off about him too. Then again, water tended to find its own level, and these guys were just freaking scary, no matter what level they were at. Still, only so much she could do.

When she heard the footsteps clumping toward her, she huddled deeper into her blanket, hoping they would think she was asleep.

But a drunken man arrived at her door, slamming it open against the wall and making her jump.

"Yeah, I figured you would be awake," he stammered, with a sneer. "It's not as if you got anything better to do with your life right now." He threw a bunch of shopping bags and a sleeping bag on the ground for her.

She stared at the sleeping bag with joy.

"Don't expect this kind of treatment all the time," he snapped. "And you better hope my buddy and I work this out, or you're likely to wind up dead." And, with that threat, he stormed away.

She wasn't sure what the hell just happened, but, as she heard more raised voices, getting louder and louder, she realized it had something to do with Bingo overhearing a comment made by Arthur about killing off his partner. And she really did have to wonder what the future held. And though he spoke with a laugh, nothing Arthur said made Bingo feel any better about his position in this deal.

"Good Christ," Arthur bellowed, "stop being such a baby."

That wasn't helping either. She didn't know how it would all end, but it didn't sound like anything she wanted to be a part of. If her captor Bingo died, that might be better, but Arthur was freaking scary in his own right, so maybe not. On the other hand, if Arthur died, she didn't have much of a chance of surviving with her other captor.

Bingo had looked like he was ready to be done with her from the start. She didn't know what was keeping her alive or why she was even a part of this deal to begin with because surely there were other ways to pressure somebody to do something.

That thought brought her right back around to Langdon. So, what was it that they wanted from the safe? Not that it mattered. If they wanted it, they would do whatever they had to in order to get it. But why Langdon and why his skill? She didn't have a clue. That was kind of a scary scenario, but nothing compared to everything else she was dealing with.

She could only send Langdon hugs and love, hoping that whatever he was going through wasn't quite so hard as what she was enduring. Now armed with the knowledge that Terk was out there and was doing something to help, she had a source of hope like nothing else. All she had to do was get better at that thread projection and bring her own energy levels back up, so that, whenever something here broke, she had the energy to jump in on the game and get the hell out quickly.

She dove eagerly for the sleeping bag, pulling off the packaging and wrapping it around her. Then she realized the other bags contained food. Whether Bingo intended it or not, it looked like it was way more than she could eat. Regardless, she collected it quickly and brought it to her side. She kept the food in the bags in case he decided to return, looking for them. Inside one, she found a bucket of chicken and just dove in.

By the time she had four pieces down, her stomach was gurgling. She wasn't sure if it was pain or joy. She only knew it had been empty for a long time. There was also water and fruit. She opened the water and gulped some down. When she realized that she would survive, her mind-set became a whole lot stronger. Now in a completely different position, she settled back and listened even more acutely to the argument still raging outside. Man, it was getting serious.

She wasn't sure exactly what was happening, but blows were dealt, from the sound of it. With that in mind, she looked at the small selection of items around her and quickly packed them up in case she needed one bag to run with. Then she ate another piece of chicken and tucked deeper into the sleeping bag. She sat here with her ears attuned, trying to listen to anything that would be helpful.

Except nothing was helpful at all.

ON THE COUCH, Langdon worked his way through the search data paperwork tied to Arthur's family, until he couldn't stand it anymore and called over to Riff, who sat beside Eton at Langdon's kitchen table.

Riff nodded, his fingers racing on the keyboard.

Taking up a position behind Riff, so Langdon could see the screen over his shoulder, he noted Riff was tracking a white van. He looked at the area but didn't recognize it. "Any idea what part of town that is?"

"Does it matter?" Riff asked.

"Yes, because we haven't been able to reach Molly in terms of telecommunications, whether by phone or via our energy, so we're assuming she's in some space where she can't use her gift."

Riff stopped and eyed him. "That's an interesting point. A few warehouses and cellars and the like are nearby, but I can't confirm where she could be yet."

As they watched the traffic cameras, following the van from one side of town to the other, Langdon pondered just what the hell Arthur was up to. "Is this Bath? Because Arthur's family has a warehouse there, or so I'm told."

Then Terk broke into his brain and announced, *I just reached her.*

At that, Langdon cried out, "How is she?"

Riff turned and looked at Langdon with an odd expression, but Riff immediately relaxed as Langdon tapped the side of his head. "Terk."

Riff rolled his eyes at that and returned to work on the laptop. "It would be helpful if he would talk to all of us."

At that, Langdon agreed. *Please tell me how she is, and I'll let the others know.*

Scared and lonely, unsure of just what's going on. I talked to her briefly, but she's also very weak. She's been trying hard to use her energy to find a solution to her problem and getting nowhere, so it's burning her out, Terk explained, his voice blunt. *We need to move up our time frame as much as we can, so that we can get her out of there in time. She also shared with me that the two guys are fighting at the moment. Something about the partner having heard Arthur say something about killing him, and now there's an all-out fight going on. She wants Arthur to win because the other guy is scary.*

At that, Langdon winced. *Wish we knew more about who that was.* Just then Riff's phone rang, distracting him. Langdon steeled himself and returned his attention to Terk. *I do need to find her, but I don't know what I'm supposed to do about Arthur's request.*

Even if you could do it, it's not something we really want anybody to know you can do.

Exactly, Langdon muttered.

Just then Terk added, *I'm hearing from Riff. I'll get back to you.*

Langdon realized just how ridiculous it was that he was sitting here in a conversation in his brain with Terk, and yet now Terk had switched over to talk to Riff, who sat nearby in Langdon's kitchen. Yet they all needed to know the same damn thing. On top of that, poor Eton had no clue what was going on. They must all look like idiots from his perspective.

Langdon groaned, picked up his phone, and dialed Terk.

When it was answered, he stated, "I'm putting this on Speaker. Cara's in my ear to conserve my energy, plus Eton is here. So let's try to keep everybody together in one conversation—the old-fashioned way."

Terk laughed. "That's fine. Rick is also surfacing, so let's give him a minute to get his brain on and come out and join you."

"Yeah, wouldn't that be nice," Langdon muttered.

"Appreciate the vocalization here too," Eton said in a mild tone, as he stretched his legs out in front of him. "A weird hum comes with your telepathic communication. Adds to the irritation for us mere humans," Eton quipped.

Sure enough, Rick stumbled out from the back room just then, rubbing the sleep from his face. "We have progress, apparently," he noted, with a smile.

"If that's what's happening," Langdon declared, "I would be happy to hear it. At the moment I'm still waiting for an update."

Riff started the conversation. "We've got DNA and a name of the second guy, this partner to Arthur," he stated, as he punched the keys of his laptop. "He's coming up on all kinds of watch lists, like Interpol, CIA, and FBI." Then he crowed, "There he is." Riff turned his laptop so everyone could see.

There was a face Langdon had never seen before, but the mugshot ID'd him as Ignatius, heavyset, and he looked like he was angry at the world and quite pissed off at whoever had taken the picture.

"I can't confirm if that's Bingo or not," Terk admitted, "but I will take as much of an image as I can and see if we can get Molly to confirm it."

"It matches the DNA that came out of the van, and the

owner has no idea who Ignatius is. It's nobody who works for him, so it just about had to be Arthur's partner who stole the van."

"That's good, because right now," Langdon snapped, "we need to find out everything we can about this asshole and see if either of them have any connections to this search area."

"Plus, is that his only partner? Arthur might have backup elsewhere," Eton shared.

The guys nodded.

"Also something is odd about the area where she's being held. It's very hard to get energy in and around it," Terk shared. "I'm still trying to come up with a solution to get around that."

"Right," Riff agreed, "and that either implies that they knew there was some way to track her, or they didn't know but assumed something was off because Langdon can get into safes, and they did this deliberately."

"That's possible," Rick acknowledged, "but it's also just as likely that it happened to work out for them this way. Good for them, bad for us. Meaning that it was completely random. I don't know that I believe in completely random, but, in this case, we don't have anything to confirm it either way. Regardless, let's go with the assumption that there's a reason for this location and that we need to follow it through on that basis."

"I'm sure there is a reason," Langdon stated. "I just don't know what it is. I don't know that his partner Ignatius has any connection to it. At least Arthur has a connection to England, and his family owned property somewhere in Bath, which is about two hours away from here. I've been trying to do a trace on that, but I'm not getting very far. The place was sold a few years back, so it doesn't appear to have any connection to him now."

"Unless it's vacant," Terk suggested. "If it is, then Arthur might know the layout very well, plus all the ins and outs. Thus he could have decided to use it, regardless of whether it was his anymore or not. Is he the kind of guy who says, *I sold it, but that doesn't matter. It's still mine when I want it?* Then that would follow."

"He's definitely that kind of guy," Langdon confirmed, hating the reminder of what this guy was like. "I swear, if he's hurt her—"

"He hasn't yet," Terk interrupted. "Let's stay focused."

Langdon shook his head. "Yeah, easy for you guys to say that. I feel that I'm not contributing anything here."

"You'll be doing something soon," Terk replied, "because you'll have to come up with a combination for the safe. I also want to put you in touch with her as soon as I can. There's something about the energy between the two of you, and I think it's costing her too."

"What do you mean?" Langdon asked, startled.

"I'm not sure what I mean at this point," Terk admitted, "but it seems like part of whatever is going on in her world, in terms of her being so cold, is also about you."

"But I'm not cold."

"No, and I'm not saying you are. I just need to talk to Cara about it first."

"Sure," Langdon muttered. "Go ahead and talk to people around me, but it would be nice if I was included."

"Calm down. When I can include you, I will," he said in a wry tone, "but we're not quite there yet." Then Terk disconnected.

Langdon wasn't sure what that meant, so he just sat back

and waited. Sure enough, Terk checked back in not too long afterward.

As soon as all were gathered nearby, the call on Speakerphone, Terk came straight to the point. "Cara says that there's an energy drain, heading outward, definitely from a female."

"Meaning?"

"Meaning that Molly's been expending a certain amount of energy all this time to help you heal. Now that she's trying to work on her own healing—and she hasn't disconnected that energy going to your healing—it's costing her. She is healing you from afar, and then exerting herself to get her energy outside of the building to reach us. That's draining her."

"Dammit. Unhook it then."

"*You* could," Terk explained, "but, if the two of you are bonded, that's not necessarily a good thing to unhook either. And that door, constructed between the two of you, and double sealed from both sides, is really not a good idea right now."

"I opened it on my side," Langdon corrected, "but it's still locked on her side."

"I think that's because of wherever she's stuck, it's draining her energy."

Langdon asked, "What would drain energy? That doesn't make any sense."

"Remember? Steel and concrete can interfere with energy, as well as mental blocks," Terk told Langdon, with a sigh. "All I can tell you is that I did meet up with her, and I think I can get back to her. She's holding on, but we need to get to her soon."

"Great, so just tell us where that location is, and we'll get right on it," Riff said, with a snort.

Terk nodded. "My team's doing a full search for any kind of steelmaking businesses, manufacturing plants, factories, even buried bank vaults, and things like that because, most likely, that's where she's at."

"Will a plant like that really have such an effect on her energy?" Riff asked.

"No such thing as certainty and all that with energy work," Terk noted. "Depending on where the kidnappers are keeping her, Molly could be in a smelter. Come to think of it, it could be she's in an office surrounded by steel. She could be in a computer server room, where they've got extra soundproof protection. Honestly … I couldn't see anything inside or out. I just felt her energy, and I followed it, and that's the only way I'll get back to her as well."

"That doesn't sound promising," Langdon murmured.

"No, it's really not. I might get a chance to see something on the way, but, as you know, I don't always see. I just go by feel. When it works, it works, and, when it doesn't, … well, it doesn't."

"Yeah, like so much of our bloody gifts," Riff pointed out. "Sometimes they're more hell than an actual gift."

"Sometimes," Terk acknowledged, "but, in this case, we're making progress. … Hang on a minute. Sounds like Tasha has found something. I'll call you back." He quickly hung up, leaving all four men staring at each other.

At that, Riff looked at the other three and nodded. "Manufacturing plants, any place with extra soundproof protection, even those walk-in vaults, you know?"

"I can help with that," Eton noted, with a huge smile, pointing at his own laptop.

"Although I don't think anything of that size, which

we're talking about, is here locally. We should look outside the city limits, but still look at Bath." Langdon reached for his laptop, then using one of his crutches, hopped over to the table and sat down. "There has to be something we can use to figure this out. Let's all think about this. … Anything that's got electromagnetic energy around it, like how about a hydroelectric plant or something along that line? Focus on places with an electromagnetic field."

"Even a large electrical plant might be enough to send her energy system crazy."

"Although Terk didn't say hers was going crazy, just that it was being damaged or interfered with or blocked or whatever."

"Right," Riff agreed. "So again, we still need to do a search here and beyond to Bath." Rick sat down beside them and worked on his laptop with them.

Just then Terk called back. "Tasha found a steel smelter. It's not running at the moment, but there are offices in it, and there has been some recent foot traffic." He quickly gave them an address, which all four men brought up on laptops.

Riff added, "It's not far away from where I had last tracked the van on the street cams." He looked at Langdon. "In Bath, England."

Langdon snapped, "Let's backtrack the movements from the traffic cams and see if we can see the van in the vicinity of the smelter."

Terk added, "We'll double-check via satellite, while you work on the street cams. I'll be in contact."

It took them another hour, but there it was. "Three days ago." Eton tapped his monitor. "The van was there."

At that, Langdon sat back and stared at him, then cried out in disbelief, "Do we really have a location?" Langdon looked from one to the other, but the men were still busy searching their monitors.

"I think we do," Rick confirmed, with a nod from Riff.

"In that case," Langdon muttered in a hurried whisper, "let's go." He hopped to his feet, grabbed his crutch, then headed to the couch and pulled out the prosthetic he'd been using. Applying the creams and powders first, he got the sock on, then quickly fitted his prosthetic and stood up, testing the feel of it.

Rick looked at him and frowned.

Langdon shook his head, catching the stares he was getting. "Oh, hell no. I'm going," he declared. "I don't know what kind of locks and security they have, but that is something … I can open up to get to her. I want her out of there."

"And if you're taken hostage?"

He shrugged. "Then I don't give a shit," he stated, not giving an inch. "In that case, it would be Arthur against me, and we've played that game way too many times. I can handle it."

"What about the safe?"

"I don't know, but, depending on where it's located, I was thinking maybe we could set up a sting. I'll go with Arthur. We'll open it up, then you can snag us on the way out."

The three men looked at each other and shrugged.

"Not a bad idea," Eton shared.

"Are you sure you can go the distance?" Riff asked.

"Oh, I'll go the distance, but I can't guarantee what shape I'll be in at the end."

Terk called, already following the conversation on the ethers. Then he added, over the phone, "Yeah, … let's hope

Cara can help you some more afterward." As the four of them quickly packed up, getting ready to head out, Terk stated bluntly, "Cara wants to warn you, Langdon. She doesn't know what she can do if that leg comes back as hamburger."

"I know that," Langdon confirmed, "but I can't leave Molly there to suffer any longer. So, if it's hamburger, I'll just deal with it."

"That'll mean more surgeries," Terk warned, "and you may not get back on your feet anytime soon."

"Maybe so, and if anybody has any spare energy to put as a buffer between my leg and the prosthetic, I'm not against it. But either way, I'm going."

"Oh, that's an interesting idea," Terk noted, with a thoughtful pause. "I'm not sure that's even doable, but, hey, the thought has been suggested."

"*Gee*, thanks," Langdon grumbled. "I was joking, but, if it's not something to be joking about, … I'm okay with it, but send all the energy you can to Molly first. I just need to go get her."

"I got it."

"Can you get a message to her?" Langdon asked.

Terk paused. "I'm not sure, but I think you should try yourself, when you get closer."

"Wouldn't that be nice? I'll see to it when I am there. We're heading out right now." And, with that, Langdon walked behind the other men, refusing to wince or give any quarter to the pain, as he focused on the task at hand. If there was ever a time when he needed all his abilities to be there for him, it was right now. As he stepped outside, he looked around. "Vehicle?"

"We're taking our rental," Riff replied. "Get in the

back.”

Refusing to take that as a slight in any way, Langdon hopped into the back with Eton, while the other two took the front. It was an older, beaten-up double-cab pickup truck. “I didn’t even know you could rent trucks like this,” he noted in amazement.

“Yeah, they are great for a deceptive cover,” Riff shared. “You don’t always want to be driving a slick late-model brand-name car. It tends to make you stick out like a sore thumb.”

Langdon hadn’t even considered that. He seriously did more desk work than fieldwork at this point, and it felt like a step down. He wasn’t even sure why the hell Terk would want anything to do with him. Yet he couldn’t have that issue on his mind today either.

He needed to get Molly back, and he needed to get his leg taken care of properly. Whatever came after that, he would deal with.

They made good time getting there, thankfully not being stopped by the authorities. The men were all silent, all focused on the job ahead. By the time they drove up to the target location, Langdon got a weird buzz in his head. “Anybody else feeling that?” he asked.

Rick looked over at him. “What are you feeling?”

Langdon frowned. “My head is full, … like somebody is trying to communicate, but I’m not getting anything clear. Like I’m not receiving it properly.”

“I’m definitely not receiving anything,” Riff shared from the front. “Maybe it’s Molly, talking directly to you.”

“I was wondering that, but it feels off.”

Rick added, “Don’t forget Molly’s energy is mixed with Terk’s right now, and it could be that Terk is trying to contact her to give her a heads-up that we're coming."

"I should be doing that too," Langdon admitted.

"Sure, you should if you can," Rick confirmed. "However, if you can't, that's just where it's at."

Langdon nodded. "I'll try it from here and see what happens." Then another thought occurred to him. "I'm just wondering if somebody else with energy is involved in all this somehow."

Rick looked at him in the rearview mirror. "Like one of the kidnappers? Like Arthur? Does he have any abilities?"

Langdon shrugged. "I really don't know. Arthur and his op is completely new and an odd deal to me." As they got closer, almost within a block away, he felt a pain at the back of his neck. "Good God," he cried out, his hands going to his neck and his throat.

Confused, Rick and Riff turned to look at him from the front seat, Eton turning in the back seat to face Langdon.

He struggled to breathe. "I think it's her," he whispered. "Dear God, let's hurry."

"What's happening?" Eton asked.

"I think that asshole has attacked her."

CHAPTER 8

MOLLY WOKE FROM a deep sleep, with hands around her throat, squeezing the life out of her. She was not able to get a grip on anything, not with him banging her head against the floor.

"Where the hell is it? You stupid bitch!"

She blinked up at her attacker, grabbing at his hands, as she tried to pull him free just so she could breathe. However, he was too strong. She was still struggling, when Arthur yelled from the door.

"Leave her alone, you idiot. You're choking her. How the fuck do you expect her to answer anything like that?"

Bingo turned, then lumbered toward Arthur, his fist swinging wide.

Arthur sighed. "You're being tiresome, Bingo. I hate it when you're drunk."

"Yeah, but you're the one who sent me out to the pub, so you knew I would get drunk." Bingo sneered. "You didn't give a shit then."

"No, I wanted you that way," he muttered. "Who wouldn't? God, this is ridiculous. You're such a bore when you act like this."

At that, Bingo took another clumsy swing at Arthur.

She sat up, pulling herself tightly into a ball, even as she struggled to breathe, frantic to clear her airways, which even now felt like they were on fire. She watched in horror as Arthur reached out with a right hook that absolutely amazed her and dropped Bingo to the ground.

Arthur sighed. "That'll keep him out of your hair for a little bit," he muttered in a mild tone. "You better hope your bloody boyfriend decides to do the right thing. Otherwise we'll have a problem." And, with that, Arthur turned to the door and walked out of the room, leaving Bingo lying prone on his face in the doorway.

She stared down at him in horror. She didn't even know why he'd woken her up from a deep sleep, but now there was no chance to even ask him. She stared out the door, wondering if she should ask Arthur. She got up and made her way to the bathroom. She hesitated in the doorway, as she stepped over Bingo, trying hard to stay out of the unconscious man's reach.

Arthur looked up and laughed at her. "While he's out, he's harmless."

"Yeah, but he won't stay that way," she muttered.

He gave her a dark look. "True, and he'll be pissed. I haven't had to knock him out like that in a while."

She didn't know what to say to that but raced into the bathroom, where she quickly used the facilities. When she stepped out, she hesitated. "What was he yelling at me about? What did he want?"

"I think you ate his chicken," Arthur replied, with a shrug.

She stared at him in horror. "I thought it was for me," she cried out. "He left it with me."

"Yeah, well"—Arthur smirked, as if he were truly enjoying himself—"he was too drunk to realize that he just gave you all the groceries, not necessarily the ones he wanted you to have."

"Oh," she whispered. "I ate some of it but not all of it."

"You better get the rest of it and put it out here, so, when he wakes up, he can at least have that much. He probably won't even remember how much he bought."

She nodded, then made her way back into her little room, and she pulled out the grocery bag with the rest of the chicken. She put it on the floor, right in front of Bingo.

Arthur looked at it and laughed. "The things that people get into a snit about." Then he left her.

She hurried back to her side of the room, as far from Bingo as she could get. As she sat back down, Arthur called out, "Have you heard from him?"

"Heard from who?" she asked, getting up and coming to the doorway again, looking puzzled.

He just gave her a bland look. "I guess that means no, *huh?*"

She frowned and shook her head. "No, I haven't heard from anybody. How could I? I don't have a phone." And, with that, she shot him a look and headed back into her room. Only as she sat down again did she wonder if Arthur had really meant what she was now beginning to wonder about.

She looked down at the still prone man in the doorway and noted his energy remained close to his body, as if, even in sleep, he was always wary. But she had seen that kind of thing before with people who had energy abilities, and it wasn't out of the line of possibility to think that Bingo did have some energy skills of his own, considering the weird sensation she'd had earlier here. Plus, the couple things that were really holding her back here. But what intrigued her the most was Arthur's comment, so she wondered if Arthur himself had abilities as well.

If so, the good guys could really be in trouble. Just no way to warn them or to know what to do about it, except sit here and wait. She pondered that, as she eyed the unconscious man in front of her, wondering if she could do something and what she could help with in this situation.

She hadn't done a whole lot with energy work because it wasn't something that she could really study or do solo. She didn't have a group, like Terk's, to give her a hand or to help teach her. It was all mostly self-taught, and then it was mostly parlor tricks. But when she learned to communicate with Langdon telepathically, she realized the real value was in keeping touch with people. And even now, as she studied Bingo, she wondered if she could possibly throw him off.

She needed to find a way to fight him that he couldn't attack. One thing occurred to her, and it almost spun her head. She could try to fill his headspace with something that would make him want to wake up, frightened enough to run away from her. She didn't know how, but she started sending dark energy toward him, wondering if that would do anything.

He shifted uneasily in his sleep, emboldening her to make another attempt. By the time she was exhausted, she had already spent a good twenty minutes working on it, and she realized that her own energy was starting to wane again. She winced at that. She hadn't considered her own energy levels because things had been looking up, so she had to put this latest experiment out of her mind. And now here she was, back in a scenario where she needed energy, and, as much as she needed it, she needed to draw on it down the road, when saving her became an even bigger issue.

Just then, the man in front of her groaned and rolled

over. He was huge, and, even rolling over, he sunk to the ground with a *thud*, his elbow and even his kneecap hitting hard on the floor. The guy had to be at least 240, and the thought of him waking up on the floor and blaming her was enough to have her curled up in the farthest corner away from him. Then she noticed the bag of chicken was gone. *Oh no.*

When he slowly sat up and looked around, his eyes adjusted even slower, as if trying to see through various layers. It made sense, and, if he were still drunk, that would be on point. At least she thought it might be. However, she wasn't so sure, not having really dealt with drunks before. When his gaze landed on her, he roared and bolted to his feet.

She cried out in fear, even as Arthur yelled at Bingo from the other room. "Leave her the hell alone."

He was still roaring, as he got to his feet and lumbered toward her.

Then Arthur came to the doorway and yelled in a threatening tone, "Don't make me knock you out again."

At that, Bingo turned, glared at him, and roared again, as he lumbered toward him.

"Remember that part about being tiresome? Now, if you want me to knock you out again, I will. But just so you know, you're starting to really piss me off."

The big man glared at his buddy, even as he shook his head, seemingly clearing his brains.

"Yeah, you need to do that a couple times," Arthur snapped, "because, right now, all you're doing is causing trouble. The least you could do is get yourself back to normal."

"You said you would shoot me," Bingo yelled. "That I was in the way and that you would be better off getting rid of me."

"Of course I said that, and I've told you why, time and time again," Arthur admitted, while sneering at his partner. "It was something I told Langdon because I have to throw him off the scent."

Bingo shook his head. "No, you meant it," he muttered.

"First, I did not. Second, even if I did, what will you do about it? Say it, what if I did?" he snapped. "Jesus, Bingo, can you just do the damn job and not get on my nerves?"

"I'm not looking after her anymore. She ate my fucking chicken."

"No, she didn't. It's out here on the counter. I see it right there."

The big man lumbered past him and presumably saw the chicken. He picked it up and stormed off, apparently satisfied with what he saw because he didn't come back into the room again.

Arthur gave her a long-suffering sigh. "See what I mean? He'll leave you alone for a while now, but there isn't much time, and we have a deadline on getting the contents of that safe too."

"You're getting it for somebody else?" she asked curiously.

He stared at her and then slowly nodded. "Smart of you. It's a private job. I just didn't want to go in there and have to bring along somebody else to open the safe."

"I still don't understand how you think Langdon will help you."

"It doesn't matter if you know or not," he replied, with a wave of his hand. "If we have to drag him down there ourselves, ... we will."

"He isn't very mobile right now."

"I know that," Arthur agreed cheerfully. "I was really hoping he had another way to do it." She stared at him in confusion, but he just waved his hand again. "Now you? .... Obviously you haven't a clue, so don't stress those pretty little brain cells." And, with that snide remark, he turned and walked out into the hallway, leaving her alone.

She wrapped her blanket around her feet, wondering if it were possible for Langdon to really do something like that from a distance. Or, even if he needed to be in person to open a safe, did he know how to do that? This was just speculation at this point, and it was a fascinating concept, yet a scary one that he hadn't shared with her.

But then a lot of his work was secret stuff and not something he could ever talk about. She curled up in a ball, pulling her knees up tight, wrapping the sleeping bag around her, trying to stave off the ever-present cold in her world, as she sent a message to Terk, hoping she didn't need to expend too much energy doing so. She needed to tell him that the deadline was looming and that they needed to act fast and that Arthur and Bingo might both have energy skills.

Almost instantly Terk came into her mind. *Listen. ... My guys and Langdon think they have a location for you,* he shared in a calm voice. *If things get dicey, stay as low to the ground and as out of the way as you can get. Follow my energy to get a message to me, as needed.* With that, he jumped out of her brain again.

She shook her head at that quick-in, quick-out thing. It was almost like her imagination at work. It might be great for him, but it left her with one thousand more questions. Still, to think that they had even tracked her this far was huge. Now all she had to do was get the hell out of here and get back to some sort of normalcy.

But, as she thought about the kidnappers nearby, their personalities, their motives, and, more so, their dark energy, she realized they would have to be put down, like the dogs they were. Otherwise there would be no end to them coming after her down the road. As long as they thought Langdon had an ability that Arthur and Bingo could exploit, they would continue to use her to manipulate Langdon. Her two kidnappers would never leave either of them alone.

She figured Terk didn't get her most recent message, so this time she followed his energy in her mind and quickly sent Terk a telepathic message to that effect.

He came back with a terse *I know.* Then he continued. *Still, we can't just go around shooting people either.*

At least he confirmed receipt of this message. Although shooting people should be allowed in a case like this. It absolutely should be allowed, Molly thought to herself. Maybe it was, or maybe it didn't matter. She wanted to think that a legion of good men were out there who could do things that weren't always within the bounds of law but still well within moral and ethical limits.

She wished that were so, that it allowed people like her to survive situations like this. The last thing she wanted was to have somebody like Arthur coming after her over the next decade. She was sure that, if he survived, she would have to look over her shoulder, wondering when that face would appear in her rearview mirror again.

The thought alone was enough to make her stomach want to heave. Of course, if she threw up here, she was pretty-damn sure nobody would clean it up or give her a hand. She would just be stuck with the mess, and they would laugh because that's the kind of guys they were. However, help was on the way, and all she had to do was keep everything status quo, just until the good guys got here.

Then she would be ready to run.

DUSK WAS FALLING, just as Riff, Rick, Eton, and Langdon drove closer to the huge smelter.

"Drop me here," Eton said, and Rick slowed the truck for him.

Eton ran to a copse of trees nearby, standing watch on the back entrance, in case anyone tried to slip out that way.

"The witching hour," Rick noted, as he drove on.

The area was fenced, but in deplorable shape, falling down in multiple sections. One of the gates hung drunkenly on one hinge, and a big No Trespassing Private Property sign hung there.

An eerie silence surrounded the place. What was probably a nice parking lot for fifty or sixty vehicles at one point in time was now completely empty. The pavement was cracked, and weeds grew through cracks in various places. It was a mess, and the building itself was deteriorating heavily, with shattered windows and rust all over the surfaces. The three men checked out this side of the smelter plant and turned at the next corner, going around the block.

"Feral dogs," Riff noted, pointing at the shadows moving in the increasing twilight. "Let me out here." He slipped out before the double-cab truck even slowed down.

Langdon frowned as Rick drove down the street and circled back. "I don't hear barking," Langdon noted. "Can he silence dogs? That could come in handy."

Rick laughed. "Riff's the on-the-spot guy, from what I hear. And, like all of us, his gifts are evolving. Yet I didn't know he was the dog whisperer." With that, Rick chuckled, then pointed, seeing movement up ahead. As he slowed the truck, Riff rejoined them, jumping in the front passenger seat once more.

Rick continued around the block, while Langdon wondered where the dogs went.

"I didn't hurt them, if that's what you are wondering," Riff told Langdon. "I'm an animal lover. ... Yet I found all sorts of booby traps in just that one field. Those old cars out there are rigged with bombs too. Terk knows, and he'll alert the local authorities to get that taken care of before some civilians or even kids are hurt. Someone wants us to take the obvious routes into the smelter. If that's what they did out here, just watch for more traps inside."

The smelter and parking lot and the grassy areas beyond took up the whole block. Langdon whispered, "It's massive."

"It is, indeed," Rick agreed.

Riff asked Langdon, "Are you any good with bomb sniffing?"

Langdon snorted. "Not my thing."

"Could end up being your thing though," Rick added, with a smirk. "Keep your mind open, Langdon. Like I said, all of us are surprised to see our gifts expanding, gaining other gifts."

"Mine are dormant," Langdon declared.

Terk's voice popped into the double cab and announced out loud, "Langdon, don't doubt any instincts that pop up today, especially while you are searching for Molly. Three heat signatures confirmed in the building."

Riff asked Terk, "Any electronic surveillance inside?"

"I can't confirm that. Either the concrete and steel of the building itself is blocking my energy or these guys inside are energy workers too. Molly seems to think so. Langdon, is Arthur gifted?"

"Not that I know of. And I don't know anything about his partner."

"Keep a lookout," Terk added. Then came silence.

Langdon frowned. "Does he project his voice like that often?"

The two other guys just laughed. Rick nodded. "You have no idea what it's like to be around Terk for any length of time."

Riff muttered, "Now what we need to figure out is where they are right now and what is our easiest point of entry."

"I brought up the blueprints," Langdon shared. "Three entrances into the place, plus the fire exits. One side has no doors."

They began their second loop around the block. They passed the first entryway, double doors with big chains across it. "That will be the least hospitable," Riff noted. They carried on around the block, traveling with the flow of traffic casually coming and going. The place was obviously an eyesore that everybody had become accustomed to, and nobody had been too worried about making changes. But this part of town was poor, after most of the industries had packed up and had moved overseas, leaving large chunks of empty buildings, making it look like an abandoned part of town all around them.

"We could each take a different entrance," Rick suggested. "Three of us, with three of them."

"A second entrance is right there," Riff noted, pointing it out. "A small door off to the side. No signs, no chains, and no evidence of anyone. That's a possibility."

It didn't take them long to locate the four loading bays all in a line, all at different heights, all along the third side.

"That's another option too," Rick added.

"Since we don't know where the three targets are, maybe we should stick together, get inside, then split up. So I would suggest the small door that we passed earlier." Riff sighed. "If not, we'll have to come in through the loading bays."

At that, Rick parked a block away in a small strip mall; then the three of them got out and headed casually toward the property. One area was heavily overgrown with bushes and trees, and they entered through that side and walked toward the small door. "Do you see any sign of cameras?" Langdon asked, as he approached the door, his hand going out instinctively, manually checking the lock, while his abilities searched on the ethers—for the first time in months. He was skeptical but encouraged.

The door was locked, but in seconds his energy pulsed through the mechanism, making a couple quick directional changes within, and popped the lock on it. Elated, he whispered, "That's better." The men heard the *click*, frowned at him, and Langdon just smiled.

Rick nodded. "You're a handy guy to have out on a mission."

Langdon nodded. "Sometimes. I was pretty handy with this stuff before, but right now? … I'm not," he muttered. "You always come up against something you can't unlock, for one reason or another, and that just kind of blows my rhythm. Keeps my ego from getting cocky."

Rick laughed. "Yep, we've had a few instances where that happens too. Even the best-laid plans, you know?"

They stepped inside, and it was all darkness here too.

Langdon looked around and whispered to the other two,

"I don't know about you two, but I assume we go forward ten feet, then six to the left, then another twelve forward."

Again Riff and Rick frowned at him, and Langdon just shrugged. "They're at the other end of that."

"Good enough," Riff muttered, with Rick grumbling in affirmation. "Let's go."

Moving silently in the vast building, they headed around what looked like large smelters with stacks of materials and equipment, all full of dust. As they followed Langdon's original instructions, he pointed out footsteps on the ground. They were literally following a track leading straight to a back room. As they approached, offices were on one side of a long hallway, with an exit out the other end.

Langdon pondered the description that Terk had given him, then whispered in a low voice, "That's where Terk came in."

Riff nodded. "I can sense his energy. It's just the ghost of the energy now, though."

"Yeah, and I can recognize the ghost of her energy to boot," Langdon muttered. "So, something is here. I just don't know how far away she is." At that, he stopped, then closed his eyes. Once again, using his direction finder, he headed down the hallway. As Riff and Rick stepped up beside him, Langdon put out his arm, pointing two fingers in one direction. "One is down there," he whispered. Then he pointed in another direction. "Two are through here."

Riff smiled. "In that case, we'll take the two, and you go after the one." They had almost made it to the point where they would split off and go in different directions, when they heard a shout, followed by a scream.

Langdon raced toward the scream because one thing he knew for sure. It was her voice. It was definitely Molly, and she was under attack.

CHAPTER 9

MOLLY STRUGGLED AGAINST her captor's big hands, clasped around her neck once more. As he gave her a hard shake again and again, her head fell to the side, as she fought for air. When he finally released her, she gulped in air and opened her mouth, screaming as loud and as hard as she could.

Bingo belted her across the face. "Enough of that shit," he yelled. "Like I haven't taken enough from you already. Shut the fuck up, bitch."

Crying but trying to hold it together, she looked around for anything she could use to defend herself. He dropped her on the spot and lumbered back toward the door.

"Wait," she called out, not knowing what she was even doing or why.

He turned and glared at her. "What? You want some more?" He glared, as he took a menacing step toward her.

She physically cringed, hating to even have him anywhere close to her, knowing she would pay for even talking to him, but her instincts had her calling out. She didn't know why, but the urge wouldn't let her go either.

"What do you want?" He sneered. "If you ask for food after you stole my fucking chicken, you should already know what kind of response you'll get."

She swallowed hard. "Fine. I'm not asking for food or

anything. I just want to know where Arthur is."

"He's out," Bingo snapped. "It's got nothing to do with you anyway."

She just stared at Bingo, hoping her silence would lead him to fill the vacuum.

"Do you really think he gives a shit if you live or die? If you do, then you don't know the man," Bingo stated menacingly. "I've seen him shoot entire families. He doesn't give a fuck." And, with that, he turned and headed back out again.

She knew Bingo was right, and she had already gathered that much. Arthur was cold, cold, cold. Nothing in his energy gave her anything to smile about, but she also knew that something was going on nearby, and she couldn't let Bingo go out there, not yet. Somehow Langdon had managed to get here. "Wait!" she called out again.

At that, Bingo turned and glared at her, his face revealing an ever-growing fury. "What the fuck is your problem?" he asked, moving toward her.

She screamed before he ever got to her, her voice loud, strong, and clear. He drew his arm back, preparing to belt her one more time, when his arm was grabbed roughly from behind. Disbelief crossed his face, and he was spun around and pummeled hard from the other side.

She gasped in shock, watching as Langdon used every trick he had to overthrow Bingo, who had to be close to twice his weight, with two good legs. But Langdon wasn't giving any quarter, and, as she watched in shock, two other men jumped in to help.

With that intervention, finally her captor went down.

She burst into tears and raced toward Langdon. He opened his arms, and, when they closed around her, she buried her face against his chest, her trembling totally out of control.

His arms closed around her securely. "It's all right," he muttered, over and over. "It's all right." Then he pulled back to look down at her. "Where is the other man? Arthur?" he demanded.

She shook her head. "I don't know. I would have thought Arthur was here, but Bingo just told me that Arthur was out."

"Got it."

At that, the other men took off, calling back to him, "Look after her."

He smiled down at her. "You're safe. It's okay. … You're safe." He lowered his head and kissed her, as she had dreamed he would during the whole nightmare of her incarceration. Her lips trembled so much, she could hardly even respond, but she wrapped her arms around his neck and squeezed him tight. When a voice came from behind Langdon, he froze, and she turned slightly in his arms to see Arthur standing there, with a smile on his face.

"Isn't that sweet." He held a gun on the two of them.

She didn't know where the other two men had gone. She stared at Langdon in horror, as he just glared at Arthur. Then she nodded toward Bingo on the ground.

Arthur turned his gun and shot Bingo in the head. The body jumped slightly once, and that was it; Bingo was gone.

Even though she had desperately wanted to get away from Bingo and had even entertained the idea of killing him herself, it was still shocking to see someone shot down in cold blood like that, even while they were unconscious. She stared at Arthur in horror. "How could you do that?" she cried out. "You don't even give a crap. He was your partner."

"Nope, I sure don't give a single fuck," he agreed cheerfully. "And just so you know. I don't give a crap about you either, so stop your sniveling and move your ass back into the other room."

She moved slowly and reached through her mind to ask Langdon, *Where are those other men?*

Gone looking for this asshole, he replied.

Amazed, she realized the psychic door between them was truly open. She almost smiled at that because, to have him here, and having that communication channel open again, was seriously wonderful. She couldn't believe how much better she felt, with his arm wrapped around her—even as much as she hated that he was here in this terrible situation. But they were in this together now, no matter what, and knowing she wasn't alone made all the difference.

That might not say much about her, but it sure revealed an awful lot about the scenario she'd been through these last few days. She glared at Arthur, as he motioned them out one door and around the corner to another room. "What will you do now?" she asked.

"I hope to confuse your friends, while I get a chance to shoot them," he admitted, with a laugh. "Of course you didn't come alone." He had a smile on his face, as he spoke to Langdon. "That would be way too simple for you." Then Arthur eyed Langdon critically. "Considering what I'd heard about the shape you're in, you're not looking too bad."

Langdon didn't reply to that, still glaring at him. "What the hell is all this BS about you wanting the numbers to a safe?"

At that, Arthur laughed and laughed. "I do need the combination because that's just easy money," he noted in a business-minded tone. "But really, apart from that combination, I want to know exactly what you're doing. I want to know how to do it myself, so I don't have to depend on pieces of shit like Bingo over there."

At that, Langdon nodded slowly. "I can almost see that as making more sense, yet not a whole lot more because generally you have another agenda that you don't let others in on. I'm not sure what else is still going on in that brain of yours, but it's not exactly something that I can teach."

Arthur's face turned red, but he had let him speak, adding another angle. "So, it's a gift."

"I don't know what to call it," Langdon admitted, with a shrug. "A nightmare, a curse, whatever. I don't have any way to control it, and I don't have any way to tell you how to do it."

"That's too damn bad," Arthur muttered, studying him, waving the gun back and forth. "Because I need something for my time and money, and I figured you would be it. I really don't like to be on the wrong course."

"I can give you the combination to the safe. *A* combination to the safe anyway," Langdon corrected, with exaggerated politeness, "but I can't possibly know for sure it will be right."

"No, of course not. I can't exactly get there anytime soon, … so it's really not a help, is it? But I'll take the number anyway."

At that, Langdon shook his head. "You're standing there, with a gun in your hand, high and mighty. What's to stop you from shooting both of us as soon as I give it to you?"

Arthur laughed. "Absolutely nothing," he stated in the same grating tone. "Except for the fact that, if it isn't the right one, I'll be back. Do you want to live with that threat over your life?"

Langdon just glared at him.

"You think you'll catch me next time, right?" Arthur asked, with a laugh. "You didn't catch me this time, so you won't catch me next time. As far as I know, your buddies have gone in a completely different direction because they didn't know about this other room here, did they? I have my own exits, secret ins and outs of this place."

At that, Langdon turned to look at the exit Arthur pointed to.

"Now," Arthur stated, "the number. Let's have it."

Langdon quickly gave Arthur a combination for the safe. Random numbers that had just rolled through his head. He had no idea if they were even close.

At that, Arthur stared at him suspiciously. "You gave that to me awfully fast."

"You did give me a bit of time to get it," he explained.

"Right." Then, as if he changed his mind, he pointed a gun to Molly's head. "Langdon, take a look at that exit and see if you think I can get out of there safely."

Langdon frowned, then turned to look, just as Arthur's gunhand came down hard on Langdon's temple. She cried out in shock, as Langdon fell over, not out cold but struggling. Arthur grabbed her and dragged her with him, yet she fought hard, kicking and screaming at Langdon for help. Langdon managed to grab Arthur's leg, and a fight ensued.

Arthur kicked hard at Langdon's injured leg, knocking the prosthetic at an odd angle, so Langdon couldn't regain his feet easily. "You're nothing but a cripple," Arthur said, laughing at Langdon's plight. With that, he was out the nearest broken window and gone.

She raced to the window, knowing that the last thing she wanted was to have this guy on her ass for the rest of her life.

LANGDON WAS UP on his feet and moving to the window, trying to see how far Arthur had gotten, but he was already out of sight. When Langdon turned to her, she fell into his arms.

"You know I get that we should probably be going after him, but I'm too damn grateful to see you and to know that I'm free."

"I get it, but all we have now is somebody who will come back after us."

She nodded. "That's good enough for me. At least, we'll have some time to sort it out," she murmured. "Right now I'm just happy to be alive. … Oh my God …" She burst into tears.

He gathered her in his arms and held her close, sending Terk a message, explaining what had just happened. Almost within seconds, the others raced toward them. Langdon barked out instructions where Arthur had disappeared, and they took off again.

Molly lifted her head and looked up at him. "You really did come with a team," she marveled.

"Came with somebody," he clarified. "They're basically Terk's men."

She smiled. "Terk is a nice man."

Langdon nodded absentmindedly. "He is. He's a good man but that doesn't make his people all that easy to deal with."

She laughed. "You know anybody who's worth their salt has to make life a little difficult for us sometimes. That's just part of it."

He rolled his eyes at that. "It shouldn't be like that. We

should just get along."

"Sure," she agreed, "but you are kind of the king of not getting along."

He glared at that, but her smile melted his heart, and he pulled her back into his arms and held her close. "Let's get you out of here," he murmured.

"Is it safe? Do you think Arthur's out there waiting, you know, with a bullet for us? For all we know, he may have another sucker, acting as a silent partner out there, with a gun too."

At that, Langdon hesitated, sending his senses out. "I think he is out there, but I'm not sure what he's doing. I think as much as anything, he's confused as to who the other men are, and so he'll bide his time, looking for another opportunity."

"I think we should give it to him, just maybe not right now …" she whispered.

"We can get this over with right here."

Molly frowned. "I just want to get home and rest, just get away from this. A shower, some food, and a little sleep would be nice too."

Putting aside his misgivings and wanting to get her to safety, Langdon smiled and tucked her up close. "Yeah, we can do that."

He proceeded to lead her outside to the vehicle. At the door, he stopped and let his senses go outward, as he assessed the danger level. "I think it's safe." Just as they went to step outside, he received a message from Terk in his head.

Don't. It's not safe. According to Riff, Arthur's still out there. Eton is searching his area, and the other two are hunting, but, so far, Arthur's on the run.

Langdon hesitated, shook his head, and shared, "Terk

says Arthur's still out there."

She winced. "Of course, and, as long as we're pigeon-holed like this, he can keep us in here."

"I think that game will get rather old very quickly," Langdon noted. "Terk's men are hunting him right now, and he knows that too."

"Maybe, but he's not a fool either," she murmured. "He's bet a lot on whatever the hell this is all about."

Langdon nodded. "I'm still not exactly sure how that works."

"With somebody like him, it isn't just work," she explained passionately. "He's got some ulterior motive going on here. I just don't know what it is. Did you see the way he shot his partner?" She shivered, remembering the dispassionate look in Arthur's eyes, as he chose the easiest option. "It's all about convenience for him, isn't it?"

"Looks like it," Langdon muttered. Just then his senses went on high alert. "I think he's swinging this way, trying to come back around on us. I need to get you out of here and back to safety," he whispered. "So, if you trust me, when I tell you to go left, you must go left, when I say go right, you must go right, okay?"

"As long as you're coming with me," she muttered, staring at him in fear.

"I'm coming," he agreed. "Arthur will be way too angry over all this to deal with right now, so, yeah, I'm coming." He gave her a smile, and, with his senses maxed out, wishing they were functioning at a much higher level, he grabbed her hand and raced out into the night, only to find absolutely nothing from his senses. They were giving nothing away, no warnings either.

He frowned, as he raced for the vehicle, got her inside,

and then sent a message to Terk. *We're in the vehicle right now.*

His response was simple and to the point. *Drive.*

And, with that, Langdon put it in gear and drove the vehicle out of the parking lot. The show was on the road now.

CHAPTER 10

MOLLY STOOD INSIDE his apartment and stared around at the surroundings that she used to know so very well. Then, after their falling out, it had become a place she wished to never see again. Yet here she was, confused, with mixed emotions, yet so much relief and joy in her heart for having been rescued from that nightmare that she didn't even know what to do. As he walked to his couch, she hated the fact that he was limping so very badly. She opened her mouth and then slammed it shut.

He turned at the couch, his lips twitching. "Yes, I over-did it. I know I'm limping, and I'm about to sit down on the couch and take off the prosthetic," he murmured. "I would suggest that you go get a shower. Some of your clothes might still be in the closet." She winced at that. "If there aren't any, just grab a T-shirt and whatever else you can find in there to wear."

She shot him a look and then nodded. "That sounds good."

"Afterward," he said, his tone firmer, "we'll talk."

"*Talk*. Yeah, we can talk." She nodded, and, not giving him a chance to elaborate, headed into his bedroom and the big en suite bathroom. In there, she stripped down, out of her dirty clothes, wincing at just how smelly and filthy she was. She turned on the hot water and stepped underneath the spray. As soon as she felt the warmth on her face, she felt the tears start. Before she had a chance to even try to control them, big ugly sobs wrenched free.

She curled up in the bathtub, with the showerhead just pouring hot water over the top of her, and she cried and cried and cried. She didn't even realize at first, when strong, warm hands wrapped around her and pulled her back against a slightly cooler body. She couldn't stop crying, still so completely out of control.

As her sobs quieted, Langdon whispered, "We better get your hair washed before we're doused in cold water." And, with the two of them sitting there, he reached for the bottle of shampoo and gently washed her hair and gently massaged the conditioner in. By the time that was rinsed out, he gave her the soap and a washcloth. "Here you go. We're about thirty seconds away from being hit with ice-cold water."

She gave a gurgle of a laugh and quickly sponged down and scrubbed off and rinsed, as fast as she could. After he turned off the water, he pulled her back against him and held her. She lay back, supported against his chest in the bathtub, and just stared up at the ceiling.

His tone, when he managed to ask the question, was thick with worry. "Did he hurt you?"

She knew he was asking if she had been raped or something similar, and she was happy she could reply with a firm no. Even though her voice was supersoft and quiet, he heard her, and his arms squeezed her gently and then relaxed.

"Thank God for that," he whispered. "I knew what you were going through, but not the details. My imagination had no problem filling in details."

"Yeah, not quite as brutal as being the one living through it though," she muttered.

"No, absolutely not," he agreed, "and I would never make that analogy. I'm so sorry this happened to you and wish I could have stopped it. I really don't know how to stop this now either. I'm afraid he'll come back again."

"I'm sure he will," she whispered. "I don't really understand what's going on or what the end of this will look like, but believe me. I'm so grateful that, for right now, it's over." She sat up and twisted to look back around at Langdon. "I'm really prone to cold right now, so, before I catch a chill, I'll grab a towel and get out."

She leaned over and found the towel she had dropped, then quickly sat on the edge of the tub and rubbed herself dry. Then she stood to find a second towel in the closet. She turned around to hand him the towel where he sat on the edge of the tub, his stump out in front, hanging there, all puffy, inflamed, and surely sore as hell. She frowned but refrained from making any comment.

He completely ignored her look, standing up strong, as he hopped on his good leg over to the counter. When he finished drying off, he motioned for her to head into the bedroom. He grabbed his crutch and hobbled behind her.

She still had her towel wrapped around her torso, and she made it as far as the bed and then just collapsed. "I did nothing but sleep, or tried to anyway," she revealed in between choking breaths. "It seemed like I slept or like I was asleep, yet not asleep the whole time," she remembered, stumbling on her own words. "And yet I'm so exhausted."

"Part of that is shock, part of it is trauma, and part of it is the adrenaline rising and then completely sliding away, leaving you in this drained state," he murmured. "You probably should just curl up and go to sleep. The bed is yours."

She sighed. "Is it that easy?"

"It is at the moment, yes," he replied. "And the sooner you get a chance to recover, the sooner we can talk about the next stage."

"Yeah, I'm not sure I'm ready for that at all," she whispered, staring up at him, tears once again forming in her eyes. She brushed them away impatiently. "You would think I wouldn't have anything left to cry about."

"It's not about crying," he explained. "It's about reacting and still being exhausted. So don't hold it against yourself. Let's just be nice, gentle, easy with ourselves, and we will get through this."

She smiled at him. "Are you sure?" she asked, with a wry look. "Together we haven't gotten through very much lately."

"No, and that's because I've been an ass," he admitted immediately. "I take full responsibility for that. I know it doesn't help much, but I do understand that I could have been a hell of a lot easier to get along with. I am my own worst enemy, and rest assured, I know that."

She gave him a nervous laugh. "Yeah, the break-up was hard on me too, you know?"

"Hey, … and you could be nice about that part," he muttered.

"No, probably not for a while," she replied. "You put me through hell."

He gave her wicked grin. "Yep, I did, and I know it, and I wish I could change it, but I can't. So we will just have to move on. If you need your pound of flesh from me, you can get it, but you'll have to dish it out in doses. Otherwise I'm not sure I can take it."

"Oh, you can take it," she argued. "I don't think I've

ever met anybody stronger than you."

"Then you haven't met very many people," he argued. "If anything, I've been an ass, and that's a weakness."

She smiled at him. "I get that we are harder on ourselves than anybody else ever is, but you do take it to the next level."

He snorted at that. "Before we get into yet another argument, lie down. You need to crash, so grab some time for yourself to just realize that you're safe, that you're here. It's over with, and we'll move on to the next stage, whatever that is. Hopefully, with some luck, we'll do it in a nice manner. I promise I won't yell and scream at you."

She laughed. "I wondered. I would very much like to believe that."

"Believe it," he declared. "Now get some sleep. I'll go out there and put on a pot of coffee."

"Why?" she asked. "You need some rest yourself. You have to be as exhausted as I am."

"I'm pretty exhausted, but surprisingly I'm holding up," he muttered, wondering about that. "I'm not sure if that's Cara's work or something else." In his head, he heard Cara scolding him. "It's Cara's work all right," he added, with a laugh. "She's busy telling me off for what I've done to my leg."

"Good," Molly stated, staring at him with a narrow gaze. "If you won't listen to me, maybe you'll listen to her. Sounds like she knows what she's doing."

"She won't really give me a choice." Langdon sighed. "Apparently I'm in danger of permanently damaging my leg."

"That's not news to you," Molly said. "You knew that before."

"Sure, I did. I just wasn't sure I was prepared to live with it," he shared simply, as if he was not talking about his leg but coffee or something. "Now I realize that there are a whole lot worse things to live without."

She stared at him, startled. "Like?" she asked, scowling. He gave her a smile so gentle that it made her heart break, then whispered his response.

"You." Then he turned and walked out of the bedroom.

She stared behind him, feeling the tears once again rolling down her cheeks. She'd spent so long waiting for him to come to his senses and to realize what they had together was real. Knowing that he was more stubborn than anybody she'd ever met in her life, yet finding them together at this point again, she smiled—something she'd never thought possible.

But he understood it. He understood them.

Finally. After all this time. Molly knew he could do and could be so many things at the top of his game, and yet there he'd been, wallowing in whatever he had deemed to be his problems. … The fact that he knew it now and was stepping up to own it was amazing. She wasn't sure whether it had something to do with this Cara, Terk, or someone else, but, however this transformation of Langdon had come about, she was seriously grateful.

He understood it. Understood *them.* As a couple. With a second chance.

She closed her eyes, and, with only the towel still wrapped around her, she laid down on the bed and whispered out on the ethers, *Thank you for helping him, Cara.* She was almost shocked when damned if a voice didn't slide into her head and whisper right back.

You're welcome. He's a hard case though.

At that, Molly snorted. *Yeah, ya think?* And then she closed her eyes and drifted off into an uneasy sleep.

OUT IN THE living room, Langdon sat down at Cara's insistence and let her get to work. After close to thirty minutes he asked her impatiently, *How does it look?*

Rough, she replied curtly, her tone angry, *but I'm working on it.*

He nodded. *You know I had to go help her.*

I know, and frankly that's the only reason I'm working on it now. If it had been for any other reason, believe me. … I would have left you to suffer the consequences of your actions.

He winced at that. *You can be quite a hard-ass yourself.*

Absolutely I can, she admitted in the same tone. *I can also see the limitations and what can and can't be done, and, all too often, it's not a case of what you can do versus what I can do to help. If I don't have your cooperation and your assistance, a lot of times I can do nothing,* she murmured. *So I can only lead you to water …*

Right, Langdon replied, *but I'll have to swim myself. Maybe now that Molly's safe, I can heal properly.*

That's the plan. Are you coming to work for Terk?

I don't think Terk wants me to work for him, Langdon stated. *Why would he? It's not as if I have all my abilities back or anything.*

You say that so lightly, yet you found her. And used your abilities in the process.

I did find her. I'm just not sure it took any abilities really. I think it was more instincts than anything. Besides, I'm pretty-damn sure I felt your energy in there as well.

After a long moment of silence, she replied, *Oh, did you now?*

But such a false, innocent sound to her tone confirmed what Langdon knew to be true. *You were using your energy to help me out, weren't you?* he asked.

She sighed. *What was I supposed to do? Let that poor woman suffer because you weren't strong enough to get out there and help her? No, of course not,* she muttered. *But I don't really want to advertise that, and I, for damn sure, don't want to have to sit here and bail you out every time you get into trouble.*

I wasn't planning on needing to be bailed out, Langdon noted, with a groan. *But the fact of the matter is, I made it because of you, and Terk will know that, whether you think he will or not. Therefore, he has absolutely no reason to hire me. Why would he want me to work for him anyway? If you guys have to help me do my job, then what's the point?*

I can speak to some of that, Terk interrupted, stepping into Langdon's head. *For one, we don't deal with the whole it's-your-job-not-mine thing. Everybody helps each other. Obviously you can do some things that we can't, but you needed some help this time to do them,* Terk explained, *and the same goes for others around here. I'm also not sure that your abilities are gone. I would really love to check it out a bit more because navigation, finding people, and serving it up as a system like that would be huge. We're always looking for people who can bring something new to the table, and it seems that half of what we do on our jobs is retrievals.*

I know, Langdon admitted, *and sometimes I can do it from a distance. No, scratch that. I used to do it from a distance.*

Why do you think your abilities are damaged now?

You mean, outside of the fact that they don't function the way they used to?

Exactly. The surgery, the trauma, your own reluctance, and the fact that you were ill is all in the open, right? What is it that you think has done that?

Several times since waking up from the last surgery, Langdon began, trying to take a calming breath, *and even before that really, it seemed as if my abilities were failing. I was really worried about it, and then afterward they didn't seem to activate at all. They were gone,* he muttered. *So, in the couple weeks since, I haven't seen any change. So, as far as I can see, I felt a little out there while searching for Molly.*

When you say gone, Cara asked, *what do you mean? Because I still feel that energy. I still feel something surging around you. I don't know what it was like before, so I can't really compare any before and after situations, but definitely still a lot of power is in here.*

My abilities were very powerful before, but I can't seem to access them now, Langdon noted in frustration. *I don't even know what that means or how it works. I don't understand it at all.*

At that, Cara replied, *Look. I'll run a few more tests. Are you okay with me doing that?*

Sure. I don't know what kind of tests you're talking about, and presumably they won't hurt, Langdon added, *but I guess if it's what you need to do, it doesn't matter if it's painful or not.*

Last time I checked, it didn't hurt anyone, she shared in a cheerful voice, *but, hey, there's a first time for everything. Just give me a few minutes.* And, with that, she disappeared.

Terk, I don't know much, but you must have had some sense of these abilities coming back online for yourself and the others, Langdon said. *I haven't had that. Can you sense anything?*

No, but that in itself is interesting, Terk noted calmly.

Let's see what Cara comes back with.

You really trust her, don't you?

Cara and her sister are healers like you've never met before, Terk declared, *and I do trust them. They're definitely people you want on your side because of the things that they can do. That's all on the up-and-up, but they also have to watch out for their own energies and abilities getting too close and getting sucked in with patients who have the ability to wreck even the healers themselves.*

Of course, Langdon agreed. *It's always been an issue with healers, hasn't it? They get too attached because they're dealing with a force of love, but then how do you detach when it's time for that person to move on?*

We've had a couple times where they've stopped people from moving on and helped them come back to life, Terk shared, *so, when I say they are healers like no other, I really mean it.*

Langdon stared around the room, not even sure what to say to that. *Is that even possible?* Then he went silent for a moment, before he went on. *I don't even know how to say this, but presumably the people that they helped were ones who wanted to come back, right?*

Terk laughed. *Yes, absolutely. Sometimes people are really drained and deep in a coma and just don't have a way to come back, and their body is suffering so severely from being motionless for so long,* he explained, trying to simplify it. *It takes time to get them back, and sometimes they're not even sure whether they're going forward or backward, and it takes somebody like Cara and her sister, Clary, to do a death walk and to help them come back from the other side.*

Absolutely amazing, Langdon murmured.

I know. I do know that, Terk acknowledged. *And believe me. After listening to some of the stories they have to tell, even I am dazzled. They don't talk about it a whole lot, but they've been through hell and back when it comes to the patients they care about. Some have chosen to go to the other side, and others have asked for as much help as possible to help them heal. Regardless, either way, when the job is done, the twin healers walk away clean. They are that good.*

Still, that would be incredibly difficult, Langdon noted. *I can't imagine losing my heart to a patient and then finding out that the time was just over.*

Exactly. But that's also why, when Cara tells you that she knows what she's doing, you have to just believe her and trust her lead.

I get it, but what am I supposed to do when it comes to sav-ing the life of somebody like Molly? he whispered. Just then Cara came back, so he had to drop the question.

So, Cara began in a confused tone. *The energy is still there, and it's still fully functioning. The reason you're not fully accessing it or at least my theory is something I hadn't considered before. You have a prosthetic, right?*

Yes, he confirmed.

But it's not on right now I presume, not with the stump so severely swollen.

Right, he said. *So what has that got to do with my energy?*

You also have pins inside you now, don't you?

Yes, I do. A couple pins, a bunch of screws, and a few bolts. You know, a whole handful of hardware was required to put me back together again.

At that, Terk started to laugh.

What's so funny? Langdon asked in confusion.

What she's saying is that's exactly what the problem is, Terk pointed out in a reassuring voice. *It's messing up your signals. The metal is directing your signals elsewhere. Or at least running them around in circles, or whatever is happening in your particular case. We've found in the past that metal has the ability to mess up our abilities, like nothing else.*

Yet it should be a conductor, Langdon argued. *So I don't understand why it would mess things up.*

It's not that your power is inaccessible. It's just that you have to find a way to ... How do I say it? ... Work with the metal, Cara chipped in. *So, in your case, find a way to work with that metal, and you should have your full faculties back.*

How does one find a way to work with the metal, when you didn't even realize it was causing a problem? he asked, completely bewildered.

That's something you'll have to figure out on your own, Terk replied. *So, I'm sorry, and I know it sounds like a complete cop-out on our part, but that isn't what we're intending at all. I can tell you an awful lot can be said for getting to know this new body of yours. Also there's a good chance that part of it is feeling very disconnected because of these metal pieces. Therefore, as soon as you get those pieces back in sync with the rest of you—accept those pins, screws, and bolts as a vital part of your body—and you'll find that everything will begin to function normally again.*

You really think so? Langdon asked. *Even if I had circled around that as causing the problem, I never would have thought that accepting my bionic parts could also be the fix for what was going on.*

Right, and, from your perspective, it isn't any different, but from the perspective of your body, it is. Honestly, if you figure out how to make that happen, chances are very good that you'll be quite a bit stronger and more capable, just because you've had to do a workaround. Workarounds have a way of building skills, so you might want to keep that in mind.

It would be great if anything is there as far as extra skills to be had, Langdon muttered. *Getting back what I had would be amazing, and, if there is more to potentially be had, that's even better.*

It is possible, but it'll all have to come from inside you, Cara stated. *As far as your current healing goes, I want you off that leg, with absolutely no walking on that prosthetic for at least a couple days. Do you hear me?*

Yeah, I hear you. Langdon sighed. *I've got my crutch beside me. I promise that, apart from emergencies or any other headaches or panics, I will use the crutches.*

I guess that is the best I can get from you, Cara grumbled, *and presumably I'll have a good idea if you end up in trouble again.*

I sure hope we don't, he murmured. *Unrealistic maybe, but I'm hoping we're past it now.*

We're not so sure about that. We still have to find Arthur, right, Terk? she murmured.

Yes, that is a definite concern. So far, we have no lead on Arthur. We think he used the sewage tunnels beside the smelter facility to escape, and my team is watching, via satellites and street cams, but there are so many points of ingress and egress to the sewer that it just complicates our search. Plus, we have no confirmation that is where he went either. Anyway I do have an energy field on your apartment, Langdon, so it will alert you and me, should anybody breach it. Plus, we are watching for any safecracking going on too. Apart from Arthur, everything else is still good. Until we know where Arthur's at and what he's up to, there's always a chance he will turn up again. With that warning, they said their goodbyes and were gone.

Langdon got up, using his crutches, then headed toward the kitchen. He crossed the room and put on a pot of coffee.

He'd meant to do it earlier but had gotten sidetracked. Having Molly safe, warmed up, and now resting in bed was a relief. Now, with the information from Cara that he didn't even know what to do with, he sat down for a moment. Knowing the truth was only half the issue, and now he felt restless and needed to move around. Yet moving around would only hurt his leg, so the best thing to do was to sit down and relax, but he just couldn't do it. He was too keyed up.

He also hadn't heard from Riff or Rick or even Eton. They were all together, he assumed. Surely they had something to report. He quickly sent Rick a text, asking where he was and if they'd made any progress.

He got a response almost immediately. They'd run out of leads and dead ends to chase, so they were headed to his place.

With that, Langdon nodded to himself. Go figure. The sense of peace he'd felt earlier was clouding quickly, which meant that they hadn't gotten as far as they needed to get, and that was a problem. With the coffee on and knowing they would arrive in just a few minutes, he got up to go to the bathroom.

A few minutes later, as he stepped out of the bathroom, a blow came out of nowhere, striking him on the side of his head, and down he went. He didn't have time to even register who it was. Only the pain stabbing at his head, followed by a kick that hit him on his already injured stump. He felt like his whole body just exploded as waves of pain washed over him, and he lost consciousness.

CHAPTER 11

MOLLY WOKE UP and stretched, then froze midyawn, as she opened her eyes to find Arthur staring at her. Terrified, she immediately scrambled up against the headboard, pulling the towel along with her. "Christ, where did you come from?"

He gave a negligent shrug, but she could see that he was pissed. "Where do you think I came from?" he snapped. "Hurry up and get dressed. We're getting out of here."

"And if I don't?"

"If you don't, I'll kill him," he snapped.

At that moment, she realized that Langdon was on the bed beside her, unconscious. "Did you hurt him?" she asked, scrambling to him to check for a pulse.

"I just knocked him out. Guys like that have to be put down fast. I should have done it sooner, but this was as good a time as any. I used to put them down before they had a chance to get back up, and I'll have to remember that," he muttered menacingly. "I'm damn tired of this."

"You could just let it be and leave us alone," she snapped. "Why is that so hard to do?"

"Because I don't have enough money to get the hell out of here, and that safe has some blackmail material I want to utilize against somebody else."

"Just go and get it," she muttered. "He gave you the

combination already."

Arthur laughed, as she skittered off the side of the bed and over to the closet, careful to keep the towel around her. "You think I'll trust that?"

"Why not? You know perfectly well he told you the truth."

"If he told me the truth, that's better yet, but, either way, he'll be coming along with me in order to prove it," he stated. "I won't stop until it's all in my hand."

"And, if he does that, then what?"

"Then I'll leave you alone."

"Yet you've already said that you wouldn't leave us alone," she stated pointedly. "So why should we trust you?"

"Ah, isn't that too bad," he replied, with a mocking smile. "You don't trust me."

She glared at him. "Is that really necessary?"

He shrugged, then frowned at her. "If you don't get a move on, I'll haul you out of here without clothes. Hear me?"

"That will attract some unwanted attention," she replied. "We'll see how far you get then."

He glared at her. "I'm just as happy to put a bullet through his stump and make sure he never gets a prosthetic to fit. I am fine with that. He's only half a man now, so imagine what will happen then?" he told her, with a sneer. "What the hell do you want with somebody like that anyway?"

She stared at Arthur in shock. "He's more of a man than you will ever be," she cried out. "He has heart."

"Heart does nothing in life," Arthur snapped. "What kind of an idiot are you? He's nothing but a loser, and he always has been."

"*Really?*" She shook her head, as she stared at Arthur. "Is that what this is all about? You're just trying to get back at him for something he supposedly did to you? For him being better than you?"

"No, but he did always win the game, and that pissed me off. It never even seemed to mean that much to him either, but, no matter how hard I tried, I couldn't seem to beat him. This time, I needed his help, and he wouldn't even give it willingly. … So I'll just take it, and, from there, we'll get what I need. Then I can disappear."

"Right. We already know that's not what you're prepared to do, so there's no point in cooperating at all. Go ahead and shoot us already," she cried out, almost hysterically. "Kill us both right now and be done with it." And she shoved her chin out at him, daring him to do it.

Arthur raised his eyebrows, then started to laugh. "You've got more spirit than he does, you know it?" She flushed at that. "But it still won't make a difference. You really want me to shoot you? I would, but I'll start with the soft tissue. I won't make it easy or fast. It will be painful, with lots of suffering, before I let you die."

She stared at him in horror.

"So, there is that. Now, it's your decision. I suggest you get dressed, or I'll haul you out of here as you are, and people can say whatever the hell they want. They still have to catch me, and, so far, I can't be stopped. And you better believe me. … No bystanders will help you, not while I've got a gun. I'll just pop them all as I go, if I need to. I really don't give a shit."

"That was one of the things Langdon mentioned about you, that you just didn't care about whatever was going on in the world around you. It didn't matter to you because, if it wasn't about you, you didn't care, and the world was only important if it affected your outcome." She shook her head. "I've never really understood that attitude."

"Of course not, because you're far too overwhelmed by feelings of guilt, compassion, and attachment. I am never troubled by those in the least."

"Yeah? Because you're defective," she declared but instantly realized she'd said the wrong thing.

He turned slowly to look at her, and she casually ignored him, pulling out the few items of clothing she had left behind in Langdon's apartment, still using the towel as much as she could while she started dressing. When she finally threw the towel down, as she managed to pull on a T-shirt, he sneered.

"You really don't need to cover your body. I don't care what you look like because I don't particularly like women, especially like you anyway."

"You probably don't like women at all," she murmured. "They're just things to you. They're not people. They're not anything to care about because you don't seem to care about anything."

"You just keep insulting me, don't you?"

"Isn't it the truth though?" she asked, facing him. "It's not really an insult if I'm speaking the truth."

"Why should I care about anybody's opinion?" he asked, his tone almost curious, as if he didn't truly understand the theory behind it. "People use people, so why would I care to be in the market and to be okay with being used?"

"If you weren't a user, chances are you wouldn't have people using you," Molly murmured. "It's all about give and take in life."

"Is it though?" he asked, with a laugh. "As far as I'm

concerned, it's all about take for me. As in, I get to take what I want."

"But, if that were the case, you would already have fixed whatever it is that's wrong in your world, and you wouldn't need to get whatever is in that safe or need to rely on Langdon. And, for that matter, I'm not sure that you're even after whatever's in the safe, as much as you're trying to set up Langdon for something."

Arthur shrugged. "I don't care whether you believe me or not. I have a purpose for this, and either you'll help or I'll just shoot you, and I really don't give a shit which."

She nodded. "Yeah, I figured that part out already," she stated.

He stared at her as he spoke, his tone odd. "You don't even sound like you're afraid of me."

"I've already faced that nasty-ass monster partner of yours, the one you shot dead, and he was a scary dude too, which is also why you just shot him, before you had to fight him for real. I still don't know why you put a bullet in his head like that. It obviously shows that you don't care about anything."

"Something was kind of *off* about Bingo," Arthur replied, "and I always knew that I would have to pop him one. I just hadn't really expected to have to do it quite so soon. However, he overheard that conversation where I'd said I was considering killing him for his share, and he didn't like that."

"I wonder why," she quipped, shaking her head. "Think about it. Why would Bingo be upset at the thought of you killing him, just to make your plan happen and to not share in the money."

"It wasn't really the money. Something was just weird

about him."

She knew exactly what Arthur meant because Bingo's whole energy signature definitely had tripped her up. "He probably had an ability or something. ... I don't know. You're right though. Something was odd about him."

"Right," he agreed, staring at her. "I didn't know what it was, but sometimes, when he walked past me, I felt a cold wave of energy coming around. I wasn't scared of him, but I was definitely respectful of the fact that he probably could have just blown me away, without a thought."

"So what then? You just figured you would get there first?"

Arthur laughed. "Of course. You've got to look after yourself in this world. Somebody like Bingo? ... He could just kill me without a thought."

"Yet he didn't because you were partners."

"He didn't because he hadn't got that far, but, once he got the money, he would have."

"Not if you got there first. However, you could have used the help to get whatever it is that you wanted from the safe," she suggested, staring at Arthur. "So it doesn't make a whole lot of sense that you popped him."

"Doesn't matter whether it does or not. It suited me at the time."

That was something she could believe. She wasn't sure what to do to get out of this mess at the moment, so, resigned to Arthur's wishes, she finished dressing, then walked over to place her hand against Langdon's cheek, sending a message into his psyche. *You're alive, but Arthur is here, holding a gun on us.*

"What are you doing?" Arthur asked her sharply.

She looked over at him. "I'm checking on Langdon."

Arthur frowned. "A weird hum is in the air."

She frowned. "What are you talking about?"

He glared at her. "I don't know. It doesn't matter."

And yet it did matter. It mattered in a whole different way because it seemed as if Arthur could receive messages but didn't know how to hear them or how to send them himself or something along that line. The fact that he was picking up a hum in the air pointed to him potentially having abilities. He had some spunk but was untrained and really didn't understand what he could do. The thought of him having abilities was terrifying, and she would do an awful lot to stop him from finding out just what it was that energy workers could do.

She and Langdon somehow had to get the hell out of this. She quickly sent Terk a message, letting him know what kind of trouble they were in. He immediately replied. His affirming receipt of her message was reassuring, though she wasn't sure what it would do for them, but, hey, she would do whatever she could at this point.

Wanting to distract Arthur from the subject of abilities, she took a proactive approach. "What do you want to do now? Will you carry him out?"

"I'll get some water and throw it on him." Arthur disappeared into the kitchen.

She immediately shook Langdon hard, as he opened his eyes and whispered, "I'm here."

"We're in trouble."

"I heard." He slowly sat up, looked wistfully at his stump and sighed. "Pass me the prosthetic."

She quickly handed it to him, and he was just buckling it on, as Arthur returned with a pitcher of water.

He looked at Langdon and smiled. "There you are," he

said cheerfully. "I figured as much. I don't know what she did or how she got you to wake up or if you were just playing games, but you're awake now, so that's all good. Now, put on your shoes and socks and let's go."

"Where are we going?" Langdon asked.

"Where the safe is."

Langdon nodded, didn't say anything more, quickly finished dressing, walking out to the other room and putting on his shoes, grabbing his wallet and his keys. Molly was now dressed in her grimy shoes, and, with Arthur coming up behind them, they walked out of the apartment.

ONCE OUTSIDE, LANGDON and Molly were directed to Arthur's car. Arthur unlocked it, and Langdon hopped into the driver's seat, then waited until Arthur got in the passenger side and Molly was in the back. "Where to?" Langdon asked mildly.

"Just drive," Arthur motioned, with his weapon. "I'll let you know."

With a shrug, Langdon turned on the engine and pulled out into the traffic, headed north. Almost immediately Arthur directed Langdon to make a series of turns, first left, then right, another left, and another, then out onto a highway, where Langdon was told to just drive. They continued on the same highway for what had to be at least an hour. Langdon assumed that Arthur knew their destination, and, because Langdon felt the air around him buzzing, he also assumed that Molly was telling Terk where they were.

Langdon hadn't heard any more from the rest of his team. He presumed the alarm that Terk had put on Langdon's apartment had warned the team to stand by. Surely they knew Langdon and Molly were in trouble again. They would follow them and set up the sting, as mentioned earlier. Still, Langdon didn't know if that was even possible. He hoped so, and, if he was doing active duty, that would definitely be something he would be pushing for right now, depending on where the team was and what they had for wheels. Then again, they may be on the satellite or even trying street cams to track Arthur's car, which matched with the intel the team had already located. That was another thing that made Langdon pause, but he kept following Arthur's directions regardless.

By the time the gas tank was getting low, Langdon was getting tired and needed to stretch his leg a bit. He turned to Arthur and said, "We need to stop for gas. I also need to take a leak, and some coffee would be great."

At that, Arthur snorted. "Yeah, sure, and then you can tell somebody you need help. I really don't give a shit," he stated. "However, we'll be stranded on the side of the road soon, so you better pull up at the next gas station."

After doing so, Langdon was allowed to go to the bathroom, and so was Molly. When Langdon rejoined them, the two of them stood by Arthur's car casually, but Langdon saw no sign of coffee. "No coffee? Really?" he muttered, with a headshake. "You expect me to work when my head isn't clear? I had a fresh pot brewing at home, before you decided to come in and bash me in the head."

Arthur glared at him. "I can't trust you to go in there and just get a coffee."

"Of course you can," he argued, with a snort, "but whatever." As it was, a fast-food place was up ahead, and he was told to pull into the drive-through, where he got coffee for everyone and a few burgers. And, with that, they kept on driving.

By the time he was told to pull over on the side of the road, they were among large rural estates. He didn't know the area at all, but it was a pretty nice view. "Are we getting close?" Langdon asked, looking over at Arthur.

Arthur nodded, as he searched the grounds around him. "Yeah, we're probably better off to walk from here."

"Okay." Langdon shut off the engine and got out. Not sure what the plan would be once they got up to the house, but Langdon didn't want to get separated from Molly. With Arthur waving the gun at them, they kept walking up the road, until they came to a huge gated driveway. Langdon surveyed the estate and noted, "This looks like the kind of place you would be after."

"Yep," Arthur confirmed. "This is it."

Such a note of satisfaction filled his voice, Langdon turned to face Arthur. "Do you even know what's here?"

Arthur shrugged. "I heard about it from a friend."

"A friend?" Incredulously Langdon eyed Arthur, with one brow raised. "Or was it somebody you beat the information out of?"

"It doesn't really matter how I got the information," Arthur responded coolly. "If you think about this, the other guy couldn't use it anyway, so I might as well."

"So what then? Nobody lives here?"

"Nope, nobody lives here," he stated, "but something very important is in that safe."

"If you say so."

They couldn't get through the gate, but there was no security system, so, with some effort, Arthur had Langdon boost Molly up. On the other side, she whispered, "It's all clear." So Arthur climbed over next, and Langdon climbed up behind Arthur, who kept coming between Langdon and Molly, keeping his gun at the ready.

At this point, Langdon was pretty well ignoring the gun, since not a whole lot to be done about it. It was getting to be almost commonplace. He knew it would come as a shock when that bullet slammed into him, but, hey, at the moment he was good. They walked up the long driveway, and he searched the area avidly. "It's a beautiful area," he noted, looking at the well-kept place. "Who owns it?"

"A drug cartel," Arthur shared absentmindedly. "They haven't used it for a long time. They're probably in jail." He laughed. "Several of them are, but this place … has been here for a long time."

"Foreign ownership is a huge problem these days," Molly noted, "not just in England but in the whole world."

Arthur nodded. "Of course people come in with money and buy up all the property, so that none of the locals can afford to buy anymore. Then they keep it as an investment or as a way to launder money, and, next thing you know, they're in the wind, and the property is falling into disrepair. If we're lucky, they come back every once in a while or at least hire local companies to do the maintenance, but, other than that, most of these properties owned by absentee foreign nationals are just slowly falling apart."

"Therefore, making them easy marks, right?" Langdon asked their gunman.

"They're certainly marks," Arthur agreed, with another laugh. "We'll see about *easy* when we get there."

"Of course," Molly muttered. "Now, because the owners don't belong here, and they're not really a part of our culture or communities, you don't really care, right?"

"Do you?" Arthur asked, looking over at her. "If you had any idea what was in that place, you wouldn't care about the owners either."

"In that case, maybe you should tell us then, so we know what we're getting into."

"*Nah*," Arthur said, "I'm not into that kind of sharing."

"What? You think you would have to share the bounty with us?" she asked, now laughing too. "Believe me. We don't want anything to do with it."

"You say that now," Arthur replied, with a wave of his gunhand, "but, when you see it, you'll think differently."

"No, I won't," she disagreed. "I don't give a shit what's in there. I wouldn't touch it anyway."

"Ah, right. Because you're what? ... A little Miss Goody Two-Shoes or something?" he asked, with a sneer.

"Something like that, yeah," she agreed. "I'm okay that other people own things. I don't have to own them. I don't have to take things from other people, and really I'm totally okay to not have as much as others. I don't have that sense of inadequacy within me."

Arthur glared at her for a moment, then chuckled. "You do have a mouth on you."

"Yeah, sometimes," she muttered. "Never really seems to help though."

"No, I imagine it doesn't," Arthur confirmed, "and I would think it might earn you a hand across the mouth every once in a while. Langdon, you really should keep her in line, you know?" Arthur said absentmindedly, studying the front door, as they walked up to the ashen oak entrance.

"I don't own her," Langdon replied. "She's a free person and entitled to her own opinions."

"Opinions are one thing, but mouthing off? ... Now

that's something totally different."

"Says you," Langdon snapped, glaring at Arthur. "You never did have a relationship yourself, did you?"

"No, I sure didn't. Women are nothing but a pain in the ass."

Molly laughed. "Why? Because we challenge what you say?"

"Partly that. It would really be nice if you would just know your place and shut the hell up."

"I don't, so you may as well forget it."

Langdon didn't say anything but stopped them as they got to the front door. "You know for sure that nobody's here?"

"That's what my intel says," Arthur murmured, "but, of course, you never really know."

"No, you never do," agreed Langdon.

Motioning the gun at Molly, Arthur said, "You go up and knock."

"Me?" She turned and looked at him in shock.

"Yeah, you," Arthur confirmed. "Anybody would let a woman who is broken down on the road into the house, but nobody would let in a single male."

"I wonder why," she quipped. "You're damn predators."

He laughed. "Go."

"Yeah, yeah, I'm going," she muttered. She walked up to the massive double front doors and knocked. Nothing but a hollow echo could be heard inside. After she knocked again with still no answer, she turned and looked back at them. "Seems to be empty."

"Good," Arthur declared, with a self-satisfied smile. "That means the information is good and gives me hope for what's inside."

She looked at Arthur and then over at Langdon, who was studying the front door, as if something were going on in the back of his mind. "What are you thinking?" she asked Langdon.

"I get a weird feel to the place," he muttered. "A very weird feeling."

"Is it dangerous?" she asked.

"Not sure," Langdon admitted. "I haven't come across it before."

Molly nodded. "I think we'll get to know this place a little closer than we would like to."

"Absolutely," Langdon murmured. With that, she stepped to the side, and Langdon walked up to the door, tested the lock, then did something she had never seen him do before, but he did it easily. The next thing she knew, the door swung open. He pushed it wide and motioned. "After you, madame."

She stared at him. "How did you do that?"

He shrugged. "Don't worry about it."

She wouldn't worry about it for now, but, boy, would she ask him about it when she got him alone. The fact that he could even do that, and so easily, worried her, but it was the look on Arthur's face as he studied Langdon that had her really concerned.

Watch out for Arthur, she whispered into Langdon's brain. *He didn't like what you just did.*

Oh, he liked it, Langdon argued. *However, he liked it a little too much. All he can see is how to manipulate me and then get me to teach him.*

Of course, That's it exactly. With that, she turned and walked into the big house, marveling at the beauty of the entranceway. "This place is so grand," she cried out.

"It is."

"Rein in your horses, people. Now an office is on the right-hand side," Arthur stated in a cutting tone. "Let's go." With that, they quickly moved toward the first-floor office, with Langdon closing the front door behind them. She studied the huge place, wondering if she could disappear and hide somewhere inside.

At that, Langdon concurred. *Pick a spot where you can hide. Stay inside the building, if you can. When it's time, you get there and stay there, so he can't find you. That would be best.*

And you? she asked.

Yeah, … he won't let me go quite so easily.

She pondered that. *Do you think we have any help coming?*

I would hope so. I know Terk's team knows where we are because I sent a message to Terk. I haven't heard anything back, but Riff, Eton, and Rick have got to be out there somewhere.

Let's hope they find us pretty-damn soon, she murmured. *I can't say I'm terribly impressed with breaking and entering, especially in a house that belongs to a cartel.*

That's a minor issue here, but I think it's owned by somebody or something else, he muttered. *There's a very strange energy to the place.*

I thought you didn't have your abilities.

I'm using Cara's energy right now, he confessed. *I don't know that I'll have enough of it to do what I need to do coming up, so that's a different story. Yet Arthur will never believe me after this.*

No, he won't, she agreed. *He's scary.*

Yeah, remember that part about finding a way to hide. … And, if I take a bullet, it is what it is, but let's make sure you don't.

I have no intention of leaving you here with this psycho, she snapped.

He smiled, as he turned toward her, then whispered, "I love you."

At that, Arthur snorted. "*Great*, you love her. You say that like you didn't have a big fight over something stupid, and that's why you weren't together when I found her," he declared, sneering, "Come on. Give me a break. Lover's rifts are ridiculous, and you two need to get over it."

"We already did," Molly replied. "Being kidnapped by a crazy man goes a long way to getting over something."

At that, Arthur laughed. "Yeah, well, that's a good thing, but I'm sure the next part won't be so easy or good. How do you think your lover boy will feel about mourning a dead partner he can never spend his life with?" Arthur asked in a cheerful voice. "Because, if you don't shut up and stop pissing me off, that's exactly what will happen."

She glared at him, and he glared right back. "You have no soul," she announced.

"We already went over this," he uttered in a bored tone. "Don't have a soul, don't give a crap, don't need to hear it," he repeated. "So … whatever."

She sighed. "Something is fundamentally wrong with you."

"Stop it," Arthur snapped.

She glared at him. "Fine, but it's not as if you can hide it forever."

He sighed, and Langdon looked at her. "It's all right. Just don't keep pissing him off."

She shrugged. "Sorry, just something about him makes me want to be mean," she admitted in a miserable tone.

"Never felt that way before."

"Yeah, well, everybody has a dark side," Arthur stated. "It's all I've ever seen from other people. So, all you're doing is proving I'm right, … that, under certain circumstances, everybody has a mean side. You too have the ability to hurt others."

"Everybody has the ability to hurt others, but we also have the ability to make a decision not to. Words and guns cannot be the same kind of hurt."

"Oh, so you're all about not hurting me?" he asked, once again mocking her.

"I don't know about that," she conceded, "because you're pretty easy to get pissed off at."

He stared at her for a long moment, then shook his head in disgust. "The mouth on you just blows me away."

At that, Langdon extended a hand. "Please, can we stop this?"

She subsided but stared balefully at Arthur. She still didn't want anything to do with the man, didn't trust him, and knew they would be shot themselves by the time this was over, likely left for dead in a house that nobody ever checked on.

That is exactly why I want you to find a hiding place and get the hell out of here, Langdon said in her head. *Whatever he has planned, he's only using you as leverage. You don't need to stay here and be a part of this.*

Yet you won't get out of here, she snapped.

At that he didn't say anything but walked into the office, where the safe was supposedly at. As he turned around and looked all over for a safe with no result, he turned back to Arthur. "So, where is this safe of yours?"

Arthur frowned, while glaring at the walls. "It was supposed to be in here, but it's hidden. You should be able to find it."

"Me? How the hell am I supposed to find it? You're the one who has the intel about it, right?"

At that, Arthur started waving the gun around the room. "Look around. Just get to work and look around. And, if you don't find it soon, I'll start shooting her."

Langdon turned and started tapping the walls, looking to see if anything was here.

When Arthur gave a shout of triumph a few minutes later, Langdon turned to see him standing beside a large picture he had taken down.

There was the safe all right. Langdon walked over, took one look, and mentally said, *Cara, I'll need some energy for this.*

Yeah, you got it, she whispered, *but, if you pull too much of my energy, I'll knock you out.*

He winced at that. *It would be great if you didn't. I'm really in a spot here.*

I know. I heard from Terk about the messages you've been sending. Help is on the way, but it may not come fast enough.

It never does, he muttered. *I'm supposed to open up this damn safe, so Arthur can get what he wants. However, at that point, it will get a lot more dangerous around here. I'm trying to get Molly to go hide, but she won't listen.*

That's because she loves you, and she doesn't want you to get hurt.

Sure, but I love her too and don't want her getting killed over this, he snapped.

Cara laughed. *You've got the energy. Just quit bitching and do what you need to do.*

And, with that, he stepped forward, rubbed his hands

gently together, and, in the pretext of bending over and trying to listen for the tumblers, he closed his eyes. Slowly he worked his way through the process. With Cara's energy he easily managed to get the hints of left and right, as he worked his way through the tumblers. Sure enough, it took about four minutes, and then everything tumbled into place, and the safe door opened. He stepped back and turned to Arthur, who was looking at him with a weird expression on his face. "There you go."

Arthur stared at him in shock, then quickly smoothed his features. He looked at the open safe, and his face lit up, barreling forward, even as Langdon motioned at Molly to get out the door. She quickly slipped out into the hall and disappeared somewhere. Langdon stayed behind, watching as Arthur went into the safe and pulled out everything inside, including a USB drive. Picking it up, he looked over at Langdon and nodded. "This is what I wanted."

Langdon raised his eyebrows. "Good. Now, are we done here?"

At that, Arthur hesitated. "I don't want you telling anybody."

"Of course you don't," Langdon agreed, "but who the hell will I tell? I don't even know who owns the property, and I really don't give a shit."

Arthur laughed. "I get that, but sorry, dude. With that attitude and all that positivity around you, I just can't trust you." There was almost a note of regret in his voice, seeing Langdon with absolutely no defenses anymore. Then Arthur turned to find that Molly wasn't in the room. He glared at Langdon. "Where is she?"

Langdon made a show of looking around, astonishment on his face. Then he shook his head. "I don't know. I was focused on you and the safe."

"Yeah, of course you were." Arthur groaned. "That stupid bitch."

"What did you expect?" Langdon replied. "You've done nothing but threaten her. She really doesn't want to die, and now here you are. You have whatever it is that you think you wanted, yet you're showing no sign of letting us go."

"What am I supposed to do now?" Arthur cried out. "I can hardly let her run away and tell the world what I've done."

"Sure, and, if you shoot me, you know you'll never get her back."

"Or I shoot you and I not only get her back but I shoot her too," Arthur proposed, with a smile. "She'll be a lot easier to track down if I take you out first."

"But then you can't ever use me again, can you?"

Arthur stopped to consider that. "I don't have any other jobs at the moment."

"Of course not," he replied, "but you went to way too much trouble on all this."

"What are you talking about? It worked, didn't it?"

"Maybe. However, you've been so focused on this and spent all this time, but did it ever occur to you that we could have done this the easy way? All you had to do was offer a decent payment."

At that, Arthur nodded. "I wondered about that," he admitted grudgingly. "I'm glad I did what I did though. I just couldn't take the chance, and I didn't know if the intel was any good."

"That's because you probably didn't trust whoever you got it from." Langdon shook his head. "You always did deal in dodgy characters."

"Yeah, well, I didn't really intend on my life going this way, you know?"

"No, but you also know perfectly well that plenty of money is in that safe, and whatever is on that USB drive may be worth even more. It must be enough to get the hell out and not have to do this anymore," Langdon pointed out. "But you won't, will you? Because you just don't care."

Arthur glared at him, as suddenly a commotion came at the front of the house.

A man called from the front door, "Who the hell is in my house?"

Arthur stared at him in shock. "Somebody just came home," he whispered in a harsh voice.

"Yeah, I hear that."

Arthur's face paled at the thought. Then he looked at Langdon, shrugged. "Sorry, buddy." The gun fired once, then twice.

Langdon felt the mother of all pains in his leg, as he stumbled from the first shot. His leg gave out from under him, and the second shot tugged on the side of his chest, and down he went. In the dim background, he heard roaring voices and sounds of running feet. Then Langdon descended straight into darkness.

CHAPTER 12

MOLLY HAD BARELY registered that somebody had come in the front door, shouting, when she heard the gunshots. The gunfire hadn't come from the front door though, so she knew who was at the end of those bullets. She sank down into the pantry that she had found to hide in, knowing it would be a while before anybody got here to look for her, unsure what she was supposed to do.

Terk was telling her to stay tucked away and hidden and that Langdon was alive, but he was hurt.

She closed her eyes and whispered to Cara, *If you need any of my energy, take it.* She almost felt the woman accepting and pulling on Molly's energy, taking it in a direction that had to be to where Langdon was. Molly couldn't believe that they had come so far, only to have this happen. She whispered to Terk, *I don't know who arrived.*

I don't know either, he replied, *and I can't see through you because you're hidden away, and I don't want you moving to give me better access*, he muttered. *I have both Rick and Riff on the outskirts of the property right now, so this will keep blowing up for the next little bit. Eton is guarding a different exit off the property. Stay where you are.*

Yeah, and what about Langdon?

You leave Langdon to me, Cara said in a soothing voice. *If you stay calm and quiet, I can use your energy for what I need.*

Just keep sending it toward him, and send him as much love as you can.

That's easy, she murmured. She closed her eyes and set up a mental bridge, sending as much love as she could to him. Still, she couldn't stop herself from telling him off a bit about getting hurt again, when what he needed was time to heal and to get back to being in good shape—but to have faith that it would happen.

She kept up a steady monologue, pouring love and energy in that direction, giving Cara whatever it was that she needed to keep Langdon alive. Yet part of Molly was completely disassociated and struggling over whatever was going on in the house.

It went quiet for a time, then she heard running footsteps and shouts. There was a bit of a tussle, and she thought more gunfire, but she wasn't sure. Then maybe a *thud* and another sound. Afterward, God help her, came Arthur's voice, calling out in a menacing way.

"Molly, are you here? You better come out now, Molly. I won't hurt you."

She wanted to say something nasty and, at the very least, point out how stupid he was to even think a line like that would work. "Oh, yeah, sure you won't hurt me. You just shot Langdon," she muttered under her breath. Yet she deliberately didn't send any messages in his direction because she didn't want to draw him to her.

As he walked through the kitchen, she curled up into an even tighter ball. "I know that probably sounded pretty scary, but he is fine. It looks like the owner came home," Arthur added, "but I just knocked him out. I didn't really want to kill the guy. Yet, on the other hand, I'm not even sure it's the owner." He kept talking, as if thinking that normal-sounding conversation would draw her out some-how. "It could be that he was just a security guard, and we triggered an alarm when we came in. Regardless, either way, I'll be leaving, and you don't want to be sitting here when he wakes up. Believe me, Molly. You don't want to meet anybody associated with this place."

She didn't, but she would be better off with a stranger than with Arthur, who had obviously just shot Langdon.

"I didn't mean to shoot Langdon. You know that. He tried to go for the gun, so I didn't have any choice. He might make it if you come out with me, so we can call for some help."

She just stared into the darkness, silent.

"Goddammit, you stupid little bitch," Arthur cried out. "Where are you?" Doors slammed, sounding a bit farther away. Then she heard him racing up the stairs.

She sagged slightly in relief, then heard another voice.

"Where the hell are you? Come on, you little piss ass," the stranger roared in the distance. "How dare you come into my house?" And, with that, came yet another fight. There was gunfire yet again, but she had no idea who was winning.

She groaned and whispered to Terk, *I don't know what's going on, but the other guy, the one Arthur knocked out before, is back up again.*

Yeah, I hear. You just stay quiet, Terk murmured. *The team is moving closer. Stay still and stay exactly where you are.*

That was easy. She had no intention of going anywhere until something broke, and prayed that the *something* wasn't her. She waited in the dead silence for any sign of something else and vaguely wondered if somehow both the owner and Arthur might have been shot. She didn't think that was possible or at least likely, so she hunkered down into the pantry and waited for what seemed like forever, then waited some more.

LANGDON WASN'T AWAKE, wasn't asleep. He was lost and drifting on the ethers. He heard a voice calling to him, but it wasn't a voice that he wanted to listen to. He was searching for something else and needed to find that one. He didn't know what he was searching for, but it was important. It was so important that everything else paled in comparison, and he didn't want to answer to anybody else.

He needed to find this thing, this person, but what, who it was, he had no idea. He kept searching through the ethers, feeling pain tugging and pulling at him, dragging him back from where he was. He kept fighting it, kept trying hard to keep going in the direction he was drawn to, trying to find this person. Trying to find what it was he was looking for.

Then somebody came up and whispered, *Sorry,* and knocked him out. When he came to the next time, he was still in a dream state, or at least he thought he was. It seemed so real, but everything was cast in a weird grayness, as if he was alive, yet only half alive.

You're alive, someone confirmed instantly. *And, yes, I know you're looking for her.*

Where is she? He spun around, wincing at the fiery pain, looking for the source of the words. *Who are you? Where are you?*

I'm here, the person replied. *I know that you're looking for her. Let me take you to her.*

Langdon hesitated for a moment because he had had so much betrayal in his past, so many lies and so much deceit to the point that he didn't think he could trust anybody, particularly not a person in that form. *Who are you?* he asked harshly, then faltered a bit. *And where is she?* Then he stopped because he wasn't even sure who *she* was.

Her name is Molly.

Yes, yes, Molly, he cried out, *where is she? She's missing.*

No, she's been found, the woman shared, her voice soft and gentle. *She's been found, and you were the one who found her. Let me take you to her.*

He hesitated, then took a small step toward her.

Yes, she encouraged. *Come on. You can do this.* He wasn't so sure that he could because the whole faith thing was hard for him.

I know it's hard for you, but she's here.

If she's here, then prove it, Langdon declared. *If you know that she's here, I want to hear her voice.*

After a moment of silence, then another voice, soft and gentle, whispered, *Langdon, it's me, honey. Come this way, please.*

He turned in the direction of the speaker because it came from another side. *Molly? Is that you?*

It's me, sweetie. It's me, honest.

I can't see you, Langdon admitted, fear in his voice.

I know you can't, but that's okay. Just follow the sound of my voice, and you already know how to do that. You're great at finding things.

I lost you, he replied immediately. *I lost you.*

It's okay because you found me again.

He hesitated at that. *I'm not sure. I don't know where you are.*

I'm ahead of you. You know how to find me, she said. *Just use your abilities and find me.*

My abilities? … They don't work, he cried out. *You know that.*

She took a deep breath and whispered, *So, close your eyes, go deep inside, and find that ability you've always had, and follow it. Follow it the same way as you always have. Please. Just let the joy carry you forward. You know that's all you have to do. You're just trying to find all the different parts of you, but think about it as if you found it already.*

The parts of me? he asked in astonishment.

Yes, she whispered, *the parts of you that have been lost, confused, and ignored over this series of accidents*, she explained. *You were in an accident. You have a bit less than all the body parts, but you also have extra material that you gained. It's all a part of you, and it's all there, just waiting for you to sort it out. Your body just needs to be pulled back together again. Your energy is distorted, and everything's confused*, she whispered.

I am confused.

I know, but believe me. You can do this. As he took several steps toward her voice, Molly whispered, *Yes, come on, honey. You can do this.* As he took one more step, pain slammed into him. *That's all right*, she cried out. *It's okay. It's just the metal body parts. You need to absorb them into your body, instead of rejecting them. You're so angry over what happened, and you're so upset over losing your leg that you've been rejecting the new parts on all levels. You are rejecting the surgery, rejecting the pins, rejecting everything that happened to you, and your body knows it. You've been in a state of war with your own body, but now you have to accept it all to move forward.*

He whispered. *I don't think I can.*

Absolutely you can, she declared. *I've always had faith in you. I've always believed in what you can do*, she whispered. *Now you need to have faith in yourself.*

CHAPTER 13

MOLLY SAT HERE, curled up in the pantry, tears running down her face, as she cried out telepathically to Langdon, but he was so lost. He couldn't find his way back out of the ethers. She had no idea what was going on in the house, but she was still being told by Terk to stay quiet. Quiet was one thing, but immobile for all this time was a completely different story. Terror kept her in place, but her worry over Langdon kept her following instructions. If they could help her to help him, then nothing else mattered, and she would do whatever they asked of her.

Just then the pantry door opened, and a huge man glared down at her.

She stared up at him in shock.

He grabbed her by the shoulder, pulled her out, and shook her. "Who the hell are you?"

She started to cry. "The other man, the one with the gun," she whispered, "he forced me to come here." He looked at her in astonishment. "He stole something from your safe."

At that, one of the ugliest looks possible crossed the man's face, and he dragged her with him up the stairs. "If that's the truth, then we'll get it out of him."

She was shoved into a second-floor bedroom, and there was Arthur on the ground, knocked unconscious, with a bullet in his shoulder. "Dear God, did you get the USB key from him?"

He looked at her and barked, "Search him."

"I hate to even get close to him," she muttered. "He is next-level scary, and he held me prisoner."

"Yeah? Still, you better do it," the angry man said, "because, if I get down there, I'll choke the life out of him."

"I kind of wish you would." She quickly dropped to her knees and searched Arthur's pockets, but she couldn't find the USB. She shook her head, turning back to look at the owner. "I don't know where it is."

He glared at her. "How the hell did he get into the safe?"

"The man he shot down in your office opened the safe. I snuck away. I don't know what happened afterward, but Arthur shot Langdon. I heard it happening, and I hid in the kitchen."

He bent down and, grabbing Arthur, gave him a shake. Arthur started moaning and groaning, but the gunman slammed him into a chair, then waited until he started to stir and smacked him hard in the face then dumped him on the floor. "Wake up, asshole."

Arthur blinked several times, then looked up to see that the situation had completely reversed, and now the homeowner had the gun and was glaring at him.

"Where the hell is the USB drive you took out of my safe?"

Arthur just blinked at him owlishly, then said, "I don't know what you're talking about."

"Yeah, you do, and I want it back."

"I don't have anything on me. Check and see."

"I did, so where did you stash it?"

Arthur noted Molly standing there. "You can't believe

anything she says. It was her idea to come here and to break in to your place."

She stared at him in shock. "Oh my God, … it was not," she cried out. "You can't listen to him. He's a liar and a cheat. He kidnapped me from my place and held me hostage for days, all to get that poor man he shot. He held me captive as leverage to make that man come here and break into your safe, and then he shot him," she cried out. "If he doesn't have the drive on him, he hid it somewhere nearby. He heard you come in and probably panicked."

At that, Arthur glared at her. "Why would anybody listen to you?" he asked, with a snort. "You're nothing."

"I may be nothing in your eyes," she stated, "but I don't go around shooting my friends and partners."

At that, the homeowner frowned at him. "Is that what he's like?"

"Yeah, you're not kidding," Molly stated, "and, if he gets that gun, believe me. He will shoot you dead. I would be next, then whoever gets in his way."

The homeowner nodded. "Good thing he's not getting the gun then, isn't it? So … I've got friends on the way. Not cops, … my friends. We'll make sure we find out where he put it."

She winced. "I don't suppose there is any chance I can go free?"

"Nope, not a chance in hell," he snapped, turning to glare at her.

"I don't mind, but can I go to my friend in the office? He's dying," she muttered, her voice barely a whisper.

"He's probably dead already," the owner stated in a cold voice. "I checked him earlier, and he didn't appear to have a pulse."

She paled for a moment, shocked. Then her arm shot outward, hitting Arthur across the side of the face as hard as she could.

"That tells me one thing," the owner shared. "Whether you are part of this or not, killing the other man wasn't part of it."

"It was never part of it," she cried out and started to sob. "Please, may I go to him?"

"Sure, whatever," he grumbled, "but, if you try to go out that front door, I will put a bullet in your back from here."

She paled, but nodded. "I won't. I promise." She quickly raced to the office on the first floor, where she dropped down beside Langdon. She reached out a hand to find that the owner was right; there was almost no pulse. For a moment she sat here in silence, but then she heard it.

So faint, it was barely there, but he was alive. It was faint to the point of being nearly nonexistent. She dropped her head against his chest and whispered, "Please, Langdon, please fight this. … I don't think I can do this alone." When she looked up, Arthur was being forced into the office and pushed into a chair. She glared at him. "You didn't have to shoot him."

"What else was I to do? He would tell."

"Yeah? And you got caught anyway. Is your intel always wrong? The owner is right here. Did you not even check to verify that he lived out of the country?"

"I didn't give a shit," Arthur admitted, then turned to the big man. "I don't have what was in the safe. She took it."

"Yeah? And when did I do that?" The bitterness in her voice was obvious. "I took off because Langdon told me to," she muttered. "He said that you would shoot him, after he got you into that safe, and there was nothing I could do."

"At least he knew what was coming," Arthur pointed out. "If you were smart, you would have left the property."

"Yeah, but I couldn't leave him alone. I only wish this guy would kill you."

"Then he'll never get the USB key," Arthur said, with a sneer.

At that admission, the gunman grabbed him by the jaw, his eyes bloodshot. "So, it was you, and you do have it."

Arthur nodded. "Sure, I know where it is, but, if I don't get out of here alive, believe me. You won't be getting it back."

LANGDON KEPT DRIFTING, pulling forward, knowing something was majorly wrong, yet it was so hard to do anything. He reached out time and time again, looking for the voices that had talked to him before, crying out that somebody should help her, that somebody needed to go after her. When a soothing voice came back through his head, he shuddered in relief. *Did you find her?* His whisper was urgent. *Tell me. Did you find her?*

Yes, we found her, the woman said. *We found her. Now you need to calm down.*

I need to help her, he cried out, pain and confusion overwhelming him.

I know, she agreed in that same soothing voice. *We're getting there. She's getting help right now, just hold tight.*

Why? Why can't I reach out to her? Where is she? It's like this black cloud is in front of me, he said. *I don't even know how to function like this.*

That's because you've been hurt. You've been shot.

He froze. *Shot?* he asked in confusion. *I don't feel that kind of pain.*

You've been shot before, so you would know that kind of pain, wouldn't you? asked the woman, with a tinge of amusement.

He stared into the darkness around him. *Yes,* he said in confusion. *Yes, I have. I was hurt, but I don't really know all the story.*

It doesn't matter right now anyway, she told him. *Plus, I don't really want your brainpower working right now. I would much rather you rested.*

He knew instinctively this wasn't the first time she'd told him that. He also knew that she had a lot of patience, but there was a limit to it.

You're right, she confirmed. *There is a limit, but you haven't come even close, and I would never get impatient with somebody in your condition. Besides, I also know that you're desperately trying to reach somebody.*

Yes, … Molly, he cried out. *Molly is hurt. She's in trouble.*

Yes, and, as I mentioned, we have people heading to her.

He shook his head, struggling to figure out a way to get her to comprehend. *Nope, no. … You don't understand. … She's in trouble now.*

I do understand, she declared calmly, *but you need to understand that you're also in trouble now. If you don't stop fighting this, we can't save you.*

He sagged back into whatever ether he was stuck on and sighed in resignation. *Are you sure somebody will get to her in time?*

Somebody is already on the way. They are headed to help her, but you need to get a grip. You need to get you out of here too.

I don't care about me, he said. *I just have to help her.*

That same gentle voice deepened. *I know that,* she replied. *Sometimes we can help everyone, and sometimes we can't. Listen. I don't want to lose you. Molly needs you, so you need to give us as much cooperation as you can.*

I'm working on it, he muttered, his voice turning grumpy, like a two-year-old.

She chuckled. *Right, and so are we, so give us a chance to do what we do, okay? You need to rest and relax and to give us a chance to get you to a point that you're stable.*

Stable? he asked, confused. *Am I that badly hurt?*

Yes, you are. You've been shot.

You already told me that, he snapped.

I did. You ignored it the first time and probably the second time too, she explained, with that same gentle amusement back in her voice.

Do I know you? I feel like I do, but I can't quite put my finger on it. I feel like I know you, yet I don't.

Let's put it this way. You do know me, she stated, *but we've never met.* He blinked at that, and she laughed gently. *I've been working on healing your system,* she shared. *You've been badly injured a couple times. We're trying to keep you alive, and you're not exactly cooperating.*

Just then he immediately remembered Molly again. *Molly is in danger,* he cried out. *Somebody needs to help her.*

Somebody is helping her, came the same patient voice. *We're not letting her die, and we're doing our best to avoid letting you go as well.*

Listen. If it comes down to one or the other, he stated, *let me go. She's special. I'm just an ass.*

At that, she burst out laughing. *I won't argue with you because sometimes you probably have been a very large ass, and you probably haven't treated her as well as you could have,* she added, her voice off. *However, I do understand why you have been treating her that way. She is not sure. I know she doesn't understand.*

No, he agreed sadly. *I didn't explain it very well. I just knew she was better off without me.*

Yeah, we've heard that a time or two, she said, with a hard sigh. *Look. I'm not exactly sure how you guys seem to think that works, but, hey, you often get into that whole mess, and it's quite frustrating.*

He frowned at that. *Did you hurt somebody too?*

No, but I understand the sentiment from other men, she noted, with a note of humor.

Oh, so it's a male thing, is it?

At that, she burst out laughing. *I'm not sure it's a male thing. Just as this reaction you're having is not good, she really should find somebody else.*

Yeah, she should, he agreed, his voice soft. *She's really special.*

You don't deserve special? she asked him.

He hesitated. *I don't know. I never felt worthy of special. So why should she put up with me now?* He was confused by that too. *Ugh, I think I'm injured,* he admitted.

You are, in many ways. You sent her away because of your injuries. You weren't healing and were getting frustrated by it all.

Right, I would have called her when I was on my feet and strong again, ... when I was a man she could be proud to be beside.

Yet she didn't ask for a man to be proud of, did she? She just wanted you to be with her, right?

I don't know, ... maybe. Then he sighed. *It doesn't mat-*

ter. … She's special.

Yeah, she is, indeed, and so are you, the woman repeated, with that touch of humor again.

You're laughing at me.

Nope, I'm sure not, she corrected, *but I do understand the human psyche a whole lot more after my years of healings. The same handful of themes come up over and over again. Where you felt you weren't good enough, so you sent her away, inadvertently making her feel like she wasn't good enough for you.*

She's more than enough, he cried out. *Why would anybody say she isn't enough?*

I think it would be much better if you let this conversation go now and just go back to bed and sleep. You can talk to her about it when you get up.

How can I sleep? How can I do that when you just said, … she felt as if she wasn't enough.

At that came a heavy sigh, and she shared, *It's because you didn't explain what was going on to Molly, and now she's out there, thinking you believe she isn't good enough, and her own psyche felt completely decimated by what you were feeling. However, now you'll both have a chance to sort it all out. I just need you to rest up first.*

And if I don't?

Yeah, that's a problem. So that's why I'll do this.

He felt a gentle wave of energy, and all of a sudden, he sank back under, blanketed by a wave that knocked him unconscious again.

CHAPTER 14

THE CONVERSATION MOLLY had tuned into was something she'd never expected to hear. She quickly called out to Cara. *Does he know I heard that?*

No, Cara replied, *he doesn't.* Then she hesitated. *But you heard it, right?*

I did, Molly confirmed, her voice soft and gentle. *He's such a stubborn man.*

I don't think he has the corner on that market, she murmured gently.

Did you knock him out?

Yes, I needed him to rest, so I could get more healing work done. He was resisting, and that's not good, she explained. Then she asked in concern. *Are you okay?*

I'm a prisoner again, and these two are fighting another round, so I don't even know what to say at this point. I'm concerned about Langdon, and all I really need to know is that he's getting out of here safely. He's on the floor in front of me at the moment, and thankfully I don't think the two fighters have noticed how different his energy is, … but to me it's very obvious.

Yes, Cara agreed. *It is a valid concern that somebody else with energy abilities might see what's going on. I'm trying to keep it to a minimum, which is another reason I needed him to calm down. He was getting really upset and anxious about you.*

I know, she said. *I heard that.*

But you didn't realize it before, did you?

He wasn't very generous with his communication, she admitted in a resigned tone. *Every time I tried to talk to him, he basically slammed the door in my face, and then I would get angry and push it further, until … you know what happened then.*

Yeah, you hit that wall. And what happens in a relationship when nobody knows how to back up and compromise, when you hit that wall, you find you don't have a relationship anymore.

And that's exactly what happened, Molly declared, *and I accept the responsibility for that too. I'm the one who pushed him and wouldn't back off. I wouldn't let him just heal on his own. Instead of letting him do things in his way and his time, I had to know what I could do to help, had to be there in his face, … trying to do something, anything, just to make him better. But nothing was making him better.*

Now you're sitting there with a gunman again. Maybe you better return your attention to that, Cara murmured. *Let me know if anybody starts noticing.*

Molly turned her thoughts and attention back to the room and the tableau in front of her. The two men were still arguing. Arthur was looking for some way to get out of this deal, whereas the owner was just looking to get his USB drive back.

She pondered where Arthur could have put that key within the house. It made sense that he stowed it away, and he had time, not a lot, but he did have a bit of time. She pondered that and then announced in a hard voice, "It might even be in this room."

The gunman looked at her. "Why?"

"Because he was in here the most. Outside of having a chance to drop it, when he heard you come in, there wouldn't have been too much opportunity for him to hide it someplace else. Maybe out in the hallway or something, but there really aren't that many options. I know that's not helpful, but—"

He looked at her. "I would send you to go look, but I can't trust you."

Her eyes widened. "Why not?"

He sneered. "Because you came with him."

"Under duress," she stated. "Do you think that gun was just here for display? I'm glad you took it off him, but you should know that he's a killer, and he will shoot you just like he shot his partner. The man was already unconscious, and he shot him point-blank, right in the head."

"He would have to get the gun from me first," the owner stated, "and I'm not quite so easy to shoot."

She assessed him and slowly nodded. "I'm glad to hear that because Arthur's tricky. I am not, so I'm happy to go look in the hallway and outside to see if I can find anything, but Arthur's not to be trusted."

The owner nodded. "The doors inside are locked, so, if you try to go out, I will know, and believe me. I won't hesitate to put a bullet in you."

She swallowed hard. "Yes, thank you. It's nice to know that, even when I do manage to get away from this asshole, I find another asshole, also prepared to shoot me at any moment."

At that, he started to laugh. "I almost believe your story."

"You should," she stated bitterly, "because it's true. Plus, who could make up this stuff? If not—"

"I'll take the chance for now, but you've been warned. Go and find me that USB key," he ordered, "and I might keep you alive."

She bolted to her feet, more than ready to get the hell away from these two. She started looking around the office, thinking Arthur hadn't had much of a chance to get anywhere else, so it had to be here. What she really needed was her lovely Langdon, the finder, who was unfortunately unconscious, fighting for his life.

She glanced down, wondering if she could use his energy and piggyback it off his ability. She sent Terk a message, asking if that was even possible.

He came back right away, an air of almost disbelief in his tone, asking if she were serious. When she quickly explained the situation, he muttered, *Good God, you are a trouble magnet.*

Yeah, tell me something I don't know. She wandered around the office, opening doors and looking for anything that would give her a clue as to where Arthur had stashed the thumb drive.

Then she stepped out into the hallway but stopped there. The gunman stepped out and joined her and asked, "What are you looking at?"

"I'm just thinking about where Arthur could have put it with the time he had. He wasn't here for very long," she said, frowning at him. "You came in the door, and I think maybe Arthur panicked and shot my friend here, but then what would he have done with the USB? He came looking for me afterward, and I think he shot my friend before that," she shared, "but I don't even know anymore. Arthur didn't have an opportunity to go very far, and he wouldn't have lost it. If there was any way he thought he could keep it, where would he have put it? It had to be quick and probably somewhere he could retrieve it on his way out."

At that, the gunman nodded. "It's the way out that's the issue, isn't it?"

She nodded. "He just wanted to steal it. I don't even know if he knows what's on it, but it was something he wasn't prepared to let go of."

"What about you?" the owner asked, glaring at her.

"I don't know what's on it, and I couldn't care less." She frowned at him. "I know Arthur won't tell you the truth, but that piece of shit held me hostage for three fucking days, thank you very much. ... I just want my life back."

Then she turned and walked over to the umbrella stand and upended it. When nothing came out, she walked to the hall closet, studying it keenly. It was still closed, but would Arthur have had time to open it and to put something inside? He had the time, but would that have made sense? With that, she went from pictures to benches, even under the benches or anywhere she thought Arthur would have had a chance to check.

As she moved forward, part of her attention was still on Langdon, lying on the floor in the office, and what Cara was doing for him. Suddenly she felt his voice creep into her mind.

Keep going, he said. *I'm trying to help.*

You shouldn't be helping at all, she whispered back. *You need to heal before you can't anymore.*

If I can't, it's too late anyway. This little bit won't make a difference, but it might make a difference in keeping you alive.

With tears in her eyes, she wiped them away, even as the gunman glared at her. "Give me a break, will you?"

He shrugged. "Your break will come, if and when you

find that key."

She nodded and kept on hunting. As she stared toward the kitchen, she whispered to Langdon, *Do you get any sense of where it is?*

Go left.

Left, left. She turned and went down a hallway. *I went left, but nothing's here.*

More left, he said. *More and more and more left.*

She groaned because more left wasn't really an option at this point. She frowned at the wall in front of her, as the gunman called out behind her.

"Did you find it?"

"No, I didn't. I'm still looking, just give me a chance."

Left came Langdon's insistent voice again.

There was no left, and then she turned around in a circle, and that put her back in the same position. He really thought something was here. She called back to the gunman. "Is there another room in here or something?"

He stared at her with an odd look, then shook his head. "No, there isn't. Why?"

"I don't know. I just get a weird feeling here." Of course that just made her sound like an idiot, but what else was she supposed to say?

The gunman turned and looked back into the office, where Arthur was still on the floor. "You really shouldn't be bleeding all over my carpet either," he mentioned in disgust.

"If you hadn't shot me," Arthur reminded him, "we wouldn't even be having this discussion."

"Or, if I'd killed you, we wouldn't be having it either."

"Then you wouldn't find what you're looking for," Arthur replied, with a sneer.

"Yeah, I'll find it, whether she helps me or not. ... Believe me. I will find it. I don't care if I have to start shooting body parts off you, but I'll find it."

Arthur shrugged. "Doesn't matter to me. It's not as if I'll have any peace and quiet on my end either way. So whatever, go ahead and shoot me."

The gunman lifted his gun and aimed.

She cried out, "Don't. … We still need him."

The owner turned to her. "*We?*" His tone was hard and cold.

She winced. "You still need him, in case I can't find it."

"You'd better find it," he sneered. "I don't have very much patience, and you're really pushing it right now."

She nodded. "I get that, and I'm sorry, but I am trying."

"Try harder," he said, with exaggerated politeness. "Otherwise I'll think that you aren't trying at all."

At that, Arthur laughed. "Yeah, that's her. Jesus, all she did was cause me trouble when I had her." He laughed. "Nothing but trouble, that one."

At that, the gunman turned and looked at him. "So you did hold her hostage?"

"Yeah, whatever," Arthur replied, with a snort. "I was trying to get the help of the guy I shot, and I figured snatching her would apply a little bit of pressure on him and get the job done."

"What then? He cracked my safe because you were holding her?"

"Exactly, but she somehow got rescued. Then I found them at his place again. This time I took both of them."

"Yeah, and I can see how well that worked out for you." When the owner turned and looked at her for confirmation, she nodded.

"As I said, I'm just trying to stay alive, trying to keep

Langdon alive."

"Find me that damn key, and you might survive yet."

She nodded and kept looking, dropping down to check under benches and anywhere she thought Arthur might have gone, but it was a huge house, and she'd never been very good at that whole hide-and-seek BS. Now, if there was any way to get Langdon conscious or at least to contact him on the other level for more detail besides just *left*, maybe she would get out of this alive. And, if she got out, maybe he could too.

But there was absolutely no way to know. At this point, it was just more of the same shit show it had been from the beginning. But she bent down and got to work, continuously moving things around, trying to find where the hell Arthur had put the thumb drive. It was just a small black key, she presumed, then realized she didn't really know what she was even looking for. She stopped, turned to the owner, and asked, "Is it like a regular key? Is that what I'm looking for?"

He looked at her, clearly confused. "I never saw it."

Arthur nodded. "It's just a small black USB key."

"Okay, good," she said. "I was afraid that, here I am, searching everywhere, and he could have it hanging around his neck or something, and I wouldn't even know."

At that, the gunman turned and looked at Arthur, who just laughed. "I told you. She's just a mess. You can see that for yourself already."

"If you held her hostage for a few days, no wonder," the owner replied, still staring. "What kind of a guy are you, that you kidnap women?"

"Hey, I needed what is on that key."

"How do you even know what is on it in the first place?" He was glaring now.

Arthur shrugged. "A guy I met in jail."

At that, the owner froze and looked at him. "Seriously?"

He nodded. "He told me about the stuff in the safe and that, because he couldn't get it, I might as well."

"How nice of you to just come help yourself."

"Yeah, I thought it could be a convenient solution," Arthur shared, with a smile. "It's not like it isn't happening all over the world."

"No, you're right. Thieves are everywhere," the owner agreed, staring at Arthur. "And all of them are pretty-damn crooked apparently."

"Yeah, but you don't need to worry about that guy anyway. He's dead."

At that, she turned and looked at him. "Bingo was your cellmate?"

He nodded. "Yeah, that was the only reason I even had a partner. He had the information I needed."

"Of course." She shook her head. "How typical of you to just kill off someone when they've served their purpose, and you don't need them anymore."

"Life is way too fun to hang around with someone with a conscience," Arthur noted, with a chuckle. "Besides, you didn't like him either."

"That guy didn't have a conscience," she stated, staring at Arthur. "He was a killer and very scary, but that doesn't mean he should have been shot like the dog he was."

"Yeah, you said it. He served his purpose. Hey, he kept you alive for a few days anyway."

"And then you shot him in the head right in front of me," she cried out, still feeling the horrors she'd endured.

At that, the gunman looked over at Arthur. "You really don't give a shit, do you?"

Arthur shrugged. "Why should I? I gambled everything on this, and, if it doesn't work, it doesn't work. There's absolutely nothing you can do about it, nothing I can do about it. On the other hand, it's a lot more fun to watch her searching for the key, knowing that she'll never find it."

"Why won't I find it?" she asked, staring at him.

"Because it's not possible."

At that, she looked over at the man holding the gun, and he was glaring at her.

"You better find it," he warned, "or find a way to get it out of this guy."

"He doesn't have a conscience," she repeated. "He would just as soon kill all of us and walk out of here."

"Oh, I understand that," the gunman agreed, waving his hand. "But what makes you think that I won't?"

Her shoulders sagged, and she went back to looking for the key. Now, if only she could get a hold of Langdon out on the ethers again and get his help. But even as she sent out a probe, she got nothing back. His earlier directions got her this far, but ahead was nothing to go on.

LEFT, LEFT. THAT was the mantra in his head.

He didn't know what it meant, but he heard it over and over and over again. *Left, left, left.*

Stop, a woman's voice cried through his brain. *Stop.*

He hesitated. *I can't stop. She has to turn left.*

That's fine, but you don't need to exhaust yourself. I can tell her to turn left, but what position is she supposed to turn left from?

He paused and groaned. *I don't know,* he whispered. *I*

just don't know.

It's important because she's in trouble now, and we need to try and help her. She's lost.

I know she's lost.

Don't start, came that same voice.

He froze, and then whispered, *I can see something.*

What do you see? The added male voice was calm and patient. There was authority in his tone, and Langdon felt like a child being chastised. *Tell me what you see.*

I see a hallway. She's in there somewhere.

Yes, she's in a hallway. I want you to step inside, open your eyes, and tell me what you see.

He immediately stepped in behind the same eyes that he had used to look down the hallway, and there was a jolt, a shock almost, and a soft gasp. Somebody sent out a *shush,* but he didn't understand. He didn't know who was playing games in his head, and then that same soothing voice washed over him.

Nobody is playing games. I want you to step inside that head and tell me what left is. Where is this person supposed to go left?

It's her. It's Molly, he cried out. *She's in trouble.*

There he goes again. The same female voice from before. *He can't seem to understand that he needs to help Molly, without getting sidetracked into this mantra, over and over again.*

I'm here came Molly's voice. It was soft, like waves, washing over him.

Molly, he whispered.

Yes, I'm here. You're here inside my head, and I need you to tell me where I'm supposed to go. You told me left, but left where?

He paused. *How can I tell?*

Look through her eyes, the male voice ordered. *I want you to teleport through her system and look through the eyes that are there and available for you. Then tell her what she needs to know.*

At that, Langdon replied cheerfully, *I can do that.* Then he opened his eyes to see a hallway that he had seen before—somewhere. *I'm in the hallway.*

Now, what is it that she needs to do?

She needs to go left.

At that, she groaned. *I am left.*

He stopped and said, *Turn more left.*

She turned more left and then more left. *Now what?* she asked in aggravation. *I'm back staring at the office.*

Go into the office, he replied. *Whatever you're looking for is still in there.*

As they went into the office, Molly's gaze landed on the body on the floor, and Langdon sucked in his breath.

Good God, that's me.

Oh, it's you all right, she confirmed. *We're trying to get us out of this nightmare. Where is the item I'm looking for?*

Langdon tried hard to focus, but it was damn hard, especially when his own body was lying there in front of him. *I shouldn't see my body, should I?"* he whispered in shock.

You can in this instance because an awful lot of people here are trying to get this problem solved, the male voice explained. *We have a team of energy workers amassing outside right now, but whatever's on that USB key is what these guys are after, so we need to secure it right now in order to get you out safely. That key is an excellent bargaining chip.*

Right. I mean, correct, he clarified, understanding. *Left.*

Molly immediately turned inside the office and stared

back at where the safe was. She walked over to the safe and opened it up.

The gunman watched her every move and snapped, "Now what the hell are you doing?"

She reached inside the still-open safe, then pulled out something and held it up. "Is this what you're looking for?"

He walked over and started to swear. "How did you know?"

"I didn't," she admitted, "but, if Arthur hadn't had a chance to get it out of here, then chances were, he'd left it exactly where it was, knowing he could retrieve it again. The safe door was closed but not locked."

The owner nodded. "Maybe that makes sense. I don't even know anymore." Then he turned and looked at Arthur, who even now was pale.

All the snide remarks had finally failed him, and he was looking like a ghost now. "So, you got it," he said to the owner. "Good for you. You may think you're special now. Like I really give a shit."

"The way I see it, you're as good as dead."

"Maybe so, but I'm not dead yet."

At that, the gunman stepped closer. Arthur, launched himself to his feet, even as Langdon watched through her eyes in shock.

Oh my God, Langdon said, *Run, Molly, run.*

She hesitated, then turned, as the two men wrestled on the floor, with Arthur desperately trying to get a hold of the gun. She raced out of the office and headed down the hall once again, back toward the kitchen.

Outside, Langdon said, *get outside.*

Where? Where's outside?

Left, turn left, he said.

What the hell? She kept turning left, following his instructions, until suddenly there was a door. She burst out and found trees ahead of her. Her feet were flying across the lawn, as she raced to get away from the chaos inside.

When she reached the first bunch of trees, someone grabbed her and pulled her deeper in. The man dragged her over to the two other men. She threw herself into his arms.

At that, Langdon whispered, *Now I can rest.* You can trust Eton." He quickly dissipated from her mind. He floated for a while, not sure what he was doing, but there was a smile in his heart, knowing that she would be okay. If she was fine, everything would be okay now. If Molly was fine, he could just rest.

Oh, no you don't, Molly cried out in his head. *I didn't go through all this to have you walk away on me now.*

I'm tired, he whispered. *I'm so tired.*

I don't give a crap, she snapped. *You fight, and you fight right now, with as much as you've got to give.*

There isn't much, he noted, his voice fading quickly.

Damn it, don't you start this BS on me, Molly muttered. *Fight!*

I am fighting, he muttered.

Don't you want to spend your life with me? she cried out.

Of course I do, but it's not to be.

Like hell, she growled, calling out to somebody named Cara and then Clary. *I need help, ladies.* And, with that, even more chaos filled his brain. Suddenly blackness took over, and he sank down into a darkness like he'd never felt before.

CHAPTER 15

"STAY HERE WITH Riff and Rick," Eton snapped. "We're going in after Langdon."

"He's on the office floor," she gasped. "He's been shot, and he's bleeding out."

"I know. We've heard from the others."

She blinked and nodded. "He's the one who led me outside."

At that, Eton turned to her in surprise, and she nodded. "We … He found the USB key. It was in the safe but left open."

"Interesting," Eton muttered, and, all of a sudden, they heard shots fired.

"Oh God," she said, sinking to the soft ground. "I don't know who the second man is, maybe the homeowner, but he was pissed that we were in there."

"Of course he was," Riff replied. "Wouldn't you be? It's his house, his property. I don't know who the hell he is either, but we have some understanding of what he's going through."

"If Arthur has the gun, we're all in trouble because he will come out shooting, or else he will disappear with that key, then come back and find us later."

"How badly hurt is Arthur?" Rick asked.

She shrugged. "I don't know. He's been shot in the

shoulder, but I couldn't tell you how bad. Nobody will waste any time with Langdon anymore because he's in such a precarious state, but everybody in there is out for themselves right now."

"Even this other guy, the owner?" Eton asked.

She nodded. "I'm not sure why he's trying to keep it safe, but that USB key was something he wanted pretty badly."

"Of course he did," Riff agreed. "It doesn't really matter why he wanted it, and it was his to begin with, so that's enough for him. And it likely matters enough to him to keep somebody silent right now, so make sure that you stay here. We'll go in, see what the hell is going on, and try to get to Langdon." At that, she sank even deeper into the brush, and he nodded. "Don't move."

"I won't," she whispered. "Please hurry though."

With that, Riff and Eton shared a glance and quickly melted into the shadows, leaving Rick at her side. She watched from a distance, hoping it was possible for them to save Langdon, but she wasn't sure anything was possible at this point in time.

The fact that he'd gone to bat and had burned through what energy he had to try and help her was huge, but she also knew that she would carry the guilt from that for the rest of her life if they couldn't save him. She could only hope that maybe they could amass enough healers to save him. He was so worth saving. She sat here, her arms wrapped around her chest, staring at the house through the brush, petrified that the wrong man would come out.

When the owner of the house stepped through the back door, he looked around for a moment, probably for her. Then he shrugged, as if to say whatever and stepped back inside. That was the first chance she had had to relax since this whole nightmare began.

Maybe, just maybe, it would be okay, but she wasn't sure because, right now, the other two guys were in there, trying to retrieve Langdon's body. Time was of the essence, and he could easily die before they got to him.

A series of shouts had her crying out softly, then she hunkered down even lower. Staring out, trying to see what was happening, a gentle voice spoke up in her mind.

Terk spoke to her. *It's all right. They're with Langdon.*

Arthur?

It appears he's been shot again. This time it's fatal.

Thank God for that, she muttered. *What about the owner?*

He's still pissed. He wants whatever the hell this is to go away, and he wants to know that you won't say anything.

I won't say anything, but he won't believe that, will he?

We're certainly hoping that we can convince him of that, but it's hard to say, Terk shared. *I want you to stay right where you are. Don't move.* And, with that, Terk disappeared from her brain.

She curled up into an even tighter ball, whispering to Langdon, *Hold on, please. Just hold on, sweetie. We'll get you. I promise we'll get you out of there.* Moments later, the softest voice ever whispered back.

It's okay, Langdon replied. *Even if I don't make it, it's okay.*

She growled, *Like hell. I didn't go through this nightmare to have you give up on me now.*

I'm not giving up, he protested, *but if I can't survive it, I can't.*

If you can talk to me, she pointed out, *you can survive this, and don't tell me you can't.*

A smile in his voice, he said, *I forgot how fierce you were.*

How could you forget? It's why you slammed the damn door on me in the first place.

Then came silence, and he sighed. *Now, if only I could go back and do that all over again.*

I don't know about doing it over again, because I really don't want to have any more of those doors slammed ever again. I thought we had something special. Then there you were, busily tearing down everything we had. That was not special at all.

No, it definitely wasn't, and, for that, I'm so sorry. I know it's not what you wanted.

Ya think? I thought we had something pure. I thought we had something that could withstand time, she wailed in anguish. *What I couldn't do was have you convinced it wasn't even worth trying for,* she'd cried out.

I know, he whispered. *I know.*

Do you? she asked sadly. *Because you're still there. You're not trying.*

After a moment of shocked silence, he asked, *What are you talking about?*

You're talking to me, when you should be quiet, building up your energy. You shouldn't be spending it saying goodbye to me. You should be saying hello to me for real, and not just in spirit form, she muttered.

I'm not even in spirit form, he told her. *I'm in telepathic form, and that's about as much as I can handle right about now.*

You shouldn't even be doing that, she stated, *so would you just knock it off and look after yourself for once? If you don't shut that door between us and heal, I will.*

Don't shut it, he whispered, a pleading note in his voice. *Please don't shut it.* She hesitated, and he added, *I promise. I'm working on the healing, and, if I make it, great. You know I don't want anything but that.*

Yeah, you tell me that, but then you keep on talking.

At that, a note of laughter entered his voice. *I promise that's the last thing, except for one more.* Then he sent her a kiss, a warm, loving smooch that she felt all the way to her toes.

She closed her eyes, feeling the tears pooling up, as she whispered to him, *I love you, Langdon. Just heal, please, just heal.*

And, with that, he was gone.

LANGDON SLOWLY WOKE from what appeared to be a near-death experience. His voice was scratchy, his throat hurt, and his body was basically in a complete shutdown. The voice in his head was reassuring, as it blanketed him. *Sorry, but I had to knock you out and put you to sleep, so we could get the last bit of healing done.*

He pondered that for a long moment. *Last bit?*

Yeah, she said, clearly exhausted. *We had to get you stabilized, and that was taking something out of us. You lost a lot of blood, but that is not so gloomy. Now, I want you to stay where you are. You're more or less conscious at the moment, but you're not allowed to get out of that damn bed, and, for the next little while, you'll need an awful lot of care,* she explained. *And there's no arguing about who is volunteering to do it.*

He smiled. *No arguing if it happens to be Molly,* he replied softly. *That would be a piece of heaven for me.*

She's here beside you and has been the entire time. So, a part of me wants to tell you to buck up, to smarten up, and to treat her the way she deserves to be treated, but I suspect that you're planning on doing that anyway.

Absolutely, he vowed, his voice soft. *How bad is it?*

Not that bad, she replied. *You pulled in and healed fairly nicely, especially considering I had to get a couple other healers in on the job to give me a hand, when it got pretty dicey.*

Did you now?

Yeah, and, for that, you owe all of us a big thank-you, she declared, but a note of humor filled her tone.

You know you have my appreciation, he replied. *Can I presume that means I'll survive?*

You will. I wouldn't take a chance on losing you now, she noted. *Molly would never forgive me, and that girl is a force to be reckoned with.*

He chuckled. *She's a fierce warrior, that one.*

She loves you very much. That is obvious.

And I love her. … I just need a lifetime now to convince her of that.

She doesn't need convincing of it at all, Cara told him, *but she certainly could use a little reassurance every now and again.*

Done, he declared promptly. *And when you say I have to stay in bed?*

Yes, you have to stay in bed, she repeated, her tone hard.

So in bed? Do I have to be alone?

At that, she gasped and then laughed. *Sounds like you're feeling better.*

I am, but I'm not exactly sure where I am.

If you open your eyes, you'll see, she said. *You've been not one of the worst cases ever, but the fact that we couldn't get to you didn't help. Not to mention that, in your efforts to try and help Molly, you were fighting against us. That didn't make it very easy on us. But outside of a little bit more healing time and more time to regain your strength, I would say you'll pull through.*

What happened to the homeowner? Arthur? The USB key?

Arthur is dead. The homeowner and the key are gone. I have no idea where but the team believes he's gone underground. The cops are going over the property but I don't care if they find him or not. He left us alive and took out Arthur. He gets my blessing.

And mine. He paused then asked hesitantly, *I guess it's not a good time to ask about the leg, huh?*

I think your leg has handled this better than you have, she murmured. *You should get a prosthetic on that pretty damn quickly.*

You think so? he asked, with hope in his tone. *You mean I won't lose more of the stump?*

I don't think so. It's holding better than you are, or at least better than you were, she replied. *I sincerely hope you're holding steady now. Anyway, I'll leave you for a bit. Please do not overdo it. If you need to get up and to go to the bathroom, definitely no prosthetic. You use a crutch or a cane. I don't care which, but do not put any weight on that leg. If you can't manage that, I guess we'll put in a catheter,* she suggested, her voice pensive.

Ah, please don't do that, he said. *It really doesn't do anything for a man's sense of being normal.*

Doesn't matter whether it does or not. You have to go to the bathroom, and I don't want any weight on that leg.

I got it, he stated. *How about I just hop?*

Remember? You've also been shot. You took one bullet in your bad leg, which was unfortunate, although we were already focused on healing it anyway. The other bullet ended up in your side, resulting in quite a lot of blood loss, which was the greatest problem.

So, I can go to the bathroom, right? Just making sure what the final orders were.

You can go to the bathroom, as long as we see you're not exhausting yourself or putting pressure on that leg. The minute we see that changing, we will order a catheter. And, with that, she drifted out of his mind.

He slowly opened his eyes to reveal what looked like a hospital room, although he wasn't sure exactly what kind of a hospital room it was because it looked pretty fancy. Then he turned his head, and, right beside him, her arm draped over the edge of the bed, was Molly.

He gently covered her hand with his. Her head bolted up, and she stared at him in shock, then cried out in joy and hopped up and gave him a gentle hug.

"I'm awake," he said. "I gather from your reaction that I wasn't expected to come out of this."

"They kept telling me that they were doing all they could," she muttered, with a shrug. "But until I could see for myself, I wasn't sure what would happen."

He smiled. "Thank you for looking after me so fiercely," he whispered.

Tears in her eyes, she bent over and gave him a gentle kiss. "We can discuss that later. All I want is for you to get home, relax, and heal."

And, since she had put so much emphasis on the word *heal,* he just smiled and nodded. "Apparently that's what my orders are from Cara too."

Molly nodded. "I can't wait until we meet them," she said, with a bright smile.

"Are we meeting them?" he asked, surprised.

"Yeah."

"How does that work?" he asked.

"I, uh, … I signed us up to go to Manchester," she declared, with a determined expression. He didn't say anything in opposition. "I'm not staying here, and now that we may have a team and more people like us," she added, "I'm all for it."

"What's in Manchester?"

"Terk, for one."

Langdon smiled. "I'm still not sure about that whole thing or my abilities."

"In that case you really don't understand what you did while you were unconscious," she stated, with a chuckle. "Believe me. I'll be quite happy to fill you in."

"And it's only because I was injured, I presume, but I don't know what else happened."

"Don't worry. I will happily clue you in, when we get to that point," she replied. "I'm sure you remember some of it, but much of it might be hazy or somewhat like a dream state."

He nodded. "What the hell was that part?" He stopped, pondering it, then asked, "Did I go into your brain and see things through your eyes?"

"You absolutely did," she confirmed. "If we go to Manchester and spend time with Terk's team, I'm thinking we'll do much more."

"Yet do we want to? Personally I just want to heal and to get back on my own two legs."

"And that's what you'll do," she declared, her voice firm. "That is the priority. Otherwise everything else is for naught."

He smiled at her. "Does that mean you and me, … that we're okay now?"

"I think I should hound you for quite a bit over the rude behavior and piss-poor attitude that you gave me," she muttered. "However, as far as I'm concerned, I was always just waiting for you to finally open that door again."

He nodded. "I'm so sorry I closed it."

She shrugged. "It's what I deserved. I was hounding you, after all."

He chuckled. "So, we're both sorry, and we're both ready to move on, together. That sounds good to me."

She curled up on his side, leaning against the headboard. "We also don't exactly have permission to get you out of here yet."

"Do I need permission?" he asked in confusion, as he looked around. "Is this a hospital?"

"It's a private hospital. Somehow you got moved here, when Riff and Rick got you out of there, with Eton's help of course."

He blinked at that. "I have some really weird memories."

"Yeah? Like what?"

"Like another gunman was there, and Arthur shooting somebody." Then he stopped and frowned. "Arthur got shot or something like that, right?"

She stared in fascination, as he gave her an outline of every detail he had remembered. When he was done, she looked at him, amazed. "I don't want to say that it's your abilities, but I think that you were either astral walking or were out of your body the whole time because you just recalled what happened after you'd been shot."

He stared at her for a long moment, then slowly nodded. "I think you may be right. Maybe we should go to Manchester."

She beamed at him. "Absolutely. I'm right about that, and I'm glad you're finally recognizing it."

He laughed, then wrapped his arms around her and held

her close.

"Now we need to get clearance to get you out of here."

"Yeah, and the sooner, the better," he stated. "I will definitely heal better if I'm not in here."

"Maybe, but they also went to a lot of work to make sure that you're doing as well as you are. I certainly won't buck those women. They're scary."

He chuckled. "Can healers be scary?"

"When you go against them, absolutely," Molly stated.

"Amen to that, I guess. I just want to spend time with you."

"Time with me sounds wonderful," she murmured, leaning over and kissing him. "We just have to make that happen."

AND HAPPEN IT did, but it took another four days before Langdon was released, and, even then, Molly didn't know where they were going. But at least Terk had a vehicle arranged for them.

"I don't want to go back to my place," she shared.

"Nope, at least not for long-term. However, for a little bit, to get away from the madness of a hospital, we could," he suggested.

"Fine," she agreed, "but I don't have any happy memories of that place."

"Neither do I," he whispered. "How about my place?"

"I kind of feel the same way about your place too. How do you feel about a motel?"

And so, from the hospital, they drove by both of their apartments and picked up a few essentials. Then they headed to a nice motel. Soon, he was settled on the couch. He looked up, smiled, and asked, "All good?"

"All good," she replied. "We can stay here however long we want, before we head over to Terk's place."

"Do they really have room for us?" he asked.

She nodded. "They do. Although I think the issue is more about how long you are likely to be laid up."

"Maybe forever. I just don't know." Then he chuckled. "Cara told me that I needed to stay in bed and off the leg. I was all okay with that, particularly if I didn't have to stay alone."

Molly sat down, blushing. "You didn't say that to her, did you?"

"Of course I did," he admitted, reaching up a finger to gently lift her face, rubbing a spot under her chin. "It is very important to know when we can make love again."

"Yeah, of course it is," she muttered. "A very important question." She gave him a headshake.

"Unless you don't want to."

She opened her eyes and stared at him. "What? You think it's only important for you?"

"As long as it's important for both of us, it's all good. I just don't want to make a wrong step."

"Ah, there is no wrong step from here on out," she noted. "I would like to think we're past all that insecurity, but obviously it'll take time."

"It might just take some good loving," he suggested, with a wicked smile.

"I can get behind that," she agreed. "I'll go have a shower. You will stay here and relax, and then I'll work on figuring out dinner when I return."

"Good idea," he said, "and, if there's anything I can do,

let me know."

"I will." She smiled, as she headed into the bathroom. She quickly had a shower, rejoicing in the fact that they were once again free, but knowing it would take time before she stopped looking over her shoulder. That was another reason she was more than eager to go to Terk's place, but she was a little concerned about how it would work in terms of how much either of them could work, but, hey, it was all good right now.

It gave them a direction; it gave them a way to train and to improve, and, if Terk had any need for their skills, she was up for it. If it meant that Langdon could do his work from home and not get into these death-defying scenarios all the time, Molly knew he would be all for it too.

After her shower, she put on a simple camisole with shorts and walked out.

He took one look, shook his head, and whispered, "I forgot how beautiful you are."

"Oh no you don't," she said. "You're still healing."

"Nope," he murmured, "I'm not, and I just got totally okayed. Cleared by my doctor too."

She stopped and stared, feeling the heat rising up her cheeks. "You didn't just ask her again?"

"You didn't believe me," he stated, "so I had to confirm it, didn't I?"

Such innocence filled his wide-eyed gaze that she groaned, feeling her cheeks flushing. "Seriously? How are we supposed to go over there, when you keep embarrassing me like this?"

"Why would you be embarrassed?" he asked, pulling her into his arms. "Do you think they aren't doing exactly the same thing? By the way, Cara and Rick are a couple. Plus, her twin, Clary, is also a healer and is also a couple with Brody, another guy on Terk's team."

"Right, so no getting away with no one knowing about our relationship," she acknowledged, as she cuddled in closer. "However, you still need to heal, as far as I'm concerned."

"Nope, I'm doing much better." And he was. He was doing way beyond *much better;* he had healed so much that it was absolutely stunning. "Besides, you mentioned *food.*"

"Right. Are you hungry?" she asked, hopping up.

He gently pulled her down beside him, then accidentally, in a big comical move, he fell to the floor and replied, "I'm absolutely starving."

She frowned at him, and then he tugged her farther down, so she was lying beside him. "I'm hungry for you," he whispered. "I'm hungry for all we've lost. I'm hungry for all the things that I thought I should walk away from. I was so angry and so upset at myself at how poorly I had done, and how poorly I had responded to treatment. Especially after being so damn sure I would bounce right back and could be the man I was before," he shared, looking at her intensely. "I know … I'm not that man, and it hurt. It hurt a lot to come to that conclusion."

"No, you're not," she whispered, "but honestly I like this one better."

His eyebrows shot up. "How can you?"

"Because this one is real," she explained, bopping him gently on the nose. "He's open, and he's talking to me, and that beats the closed-off one I had before."

He smiled, leaned over, and kissed her. "I may never get that prosthetic on."

"I really don't give a crap if you do or you don't," she

declared. "I don't care if you ever wear it. It's got nothing to do with who you are. It happens to be the body that you're living with right now, but it certainly isn't a problem for me. I feel bad that it's a hardship for you," she noted, "and I wish I could do something to make it easier, but I know that I can't, and that is a battle that I have to walk away from."

"And, for that reason, you're smarter than me," he stated, with a twitch of his lips. "Because you knew when to walk away, and I didn't."

"Yeah, well, I won't argue that point," she said, and she wrapped her arms around his neck.

"Are you serious about wanting food now or is later okay?" he asked, as he nuzzled her nose. "Like, a lot later?"

"We could order takeout, and, by the time it's here, … we might be ready for food."

"Does that mean you're hungry?"

She smiled. "I'm hungry for you," she whispered. "Anything else is just gravy."

"Well, … then I suggest we push off food until later because I really don't want to change this path we're on." And, with that, he lowered his head and kissed her passionately, as if all the months had built up to this huge crescendo of need, ready to burst from inside out. She wrapped her arms around him and held on tight, absolutely loving the way her body shivered in his embrace.

"I was so afraid we would never have this again," she whispered, "so afraid we'd lost it all."

"Nope," he replied. "I was stubborn, pigheaded, stupid, and anything else you want to call me. But I wasn't that stubborn, not so much that I would lose you. I was just holding you at arm's length, while I dealt with my own crap, and unfortunately I wasn't very fast dealing with it."

She kissed him gently again, then again and still again. "We're here now," she muttered, "and that makes it all worthwhile."

"Are you sure?"

"Positive," she murmured, "now stop wasting time." And, with that, she grabbed him by the ears and pulled him down for a sizzling kiss.

By the time he lifted his head, he was out of breath. "Christ, I'd forgotten that ferociousness."

"How could you forget?" Then she gently lifted her hips, pulsing against him. "Have you forgotten this too?"

"Never. That would be impossible." He chuckled, and this time when he kissed her, her senses fired off in all directions.

She shuddered in his arms and whispered, "Dear God, I have missed this so much." She was trembling in his arms with need.

"Still need this," he whispered.

"Even more," she muttered. "Even more. Next time we'll go to the bed, but, right now, I want you here. I want you now, and I want you inside me in whatever way it happens."

At that, he shifted, and she realized he had already taken off her camisole, and she didn't even notice. She chuckled. "I forgot how smooth you were."

"Some things are smoother than others, but, hey, we're getting there."

She placed a finger against his lips and then quickly re-placed her finger with her lips and tongue, until her thighs were spread wide, and he was poised at the heart of her. By the time he drove in once and paused, his forehead coming down to touch hers, he whispered, "I'm so sorry."

She shrugged. "Don't be. It's where we were, but it's not where we are now. We've come a long way," she whispered.

"That's true."

"We're not sliding backward. We're here now, so let's celebrate the joy of how far we've come."

He smiled and started to move. Within seconds, she came apart in his arms, while the need crashed through her, and he followed her moments later, as the two of them lay trembling on the floor.

Finally, when she could catch her breath, she whispered, "The bed would have been nicer."

"Yep, it sure would have," he agreed, "but we didn't make it."

"Nope. Next time though."

"Maybe," he replied, his breathing slowly returning to normal, "if you move fast."

She rolled her head to the side, looked at him in surprise, and he grinned. He then tackled her and then rolled back over on top of her. This time, he grabbed her arms, pulled them up over her head, and whispered. "Yes, I'm serious." And he proceeded to love her all over again.

By the time they made it to bed, the takeout food had been ordered and was on the way. Once the food was delivered, and they were already in bed, curled up together, munching away on pizza, she stared down at it, and smiled. "Do they have pizza where Terk is?"

"If they don't," he said. "We'll learn how to make it."

She chuckled. "It will be different, you know."

"It will be, but I think it will be good for us. In many ways, we've been alone for too damn long," he noted. "There has been just us. We didn't have anybody else like us, and I think that makes it even harder. We're meant to be part of a community."

She nodded. "I'm looking forward to it, as long as you're coming with me. And I wanted to say how sorry I am about your mother. It's hard to lose someone you love."

"It is," he nodded. "and I won't let it happen again. So you're not going without me."

At that, she burst into laughter and kissed him yet again. One for tomorrow and all the tomorrows to come.

EPILOGUE

R IFF SAT ACROSS the table and stared at Terk, the others quietly watching. "So, what? Did you get anywhere?"

"It's still in progress," Tasha noted, from his side. "It's not been all that easy to find information."

"That's because we're sitting here," Riff snapped, "doing nothing."

"It's true that we are here, and sitting, but we're certainly not doing *nothing*," Terk clarified. "You also know that things have to happen in their own time."

Riff glared at him. "Sounds like an excuse to me."

At that, Terk shot him a look and took a breath. "Come on, Riff. It's not an excuse, and you and I both know it."

"Yes, but I'm damn impatient."

"I know, with good cause. We're also getting a lot of phone calls from Angela."

Riff frowned at that and looked off in the distance.

"What's the relationship between you two?"

"Complex," he snapped.

At that, several people around the table laughed.

"Yeah, that's something we've all dealt with," Terk shared, with a smile. "It doesn't necessarily wash though."

"Fine," Riff grumbled. "I'll wait a little bit longer."

"And Angela?" Celia asked, patting her belly. "She seems to think she will be needed."

Riff winced.

"If she is, you would be the best bet to contact her," Terk suggested to Riff, but Riff seemed to want to be anywhere but here. "I understand that she's very, very good at what she does."

"Is she like us?" Cara asked, looking at Riff intently. He gave her a reluctant nod. "She's a healer then?" Cara and Clary looked over at Riff with interest.

"We can always use more healers." Clary liked that prospect.

"You don't want her," Riff declared.

"Why is that?" she asked.

"She'll organize your life away," he replied, with a wave of his hand. "She'll get in your face, and you won't know if you're coming or going."

At that, Cara nodded slowly. "I see."

"No, you don't see," Riff snapped, glaring. "You don't see anything."

"Yeah, I do," she argued. "I think we should probably meet her." She turned to Terk.

Terk studied Riff. "It's probably a good idea, even if it's not today. Maybe in a few days or even a couple weeks."

"That's possible," Cara noted, with a nod as she assessed the room. "It's probably good timing, but we don't want her too early."

"No, we don't, and, if she knows when to come, it won't matter what you say," Riff declared, looking at her. "She'll be here regardless, and, when you see her, you'll know you're heading for trouble."

"Trouble or just the timing of things?" Cara asked.

Riff shrugged. "I see her, and it means trouble, so who knows. It depends on the relationship you have with her," he muttered.

At that, Cara could hardly hide her smile.

Terk looked around the room, recognizing what the others also recognized but what Riff was desperately trying not to. Terk realized there would be yet another relationship happening, but it just wasn't time yet.

Terk's phone rang, and he looked down at the screen to see who was calling. "Hey, Levi. How's life?"

"Everything is fine here, but maybe I should ask you how it's going on your end."

Terk assessed it for a moment, then replied, "I would have said all is tickety-boo over here, at least for the moment. So ... why are you calling then?"

"What? Can't a friend just call?"

"Yep, you sure can. But what's up?"

Levi hesitated. "Somebody contacted me about some work, and, in my research, we came up with something that's a bit off," he shared. "I'm wondering if he isn't one of yours."

"One of mine? That would be interesting. Why? Do you think we need him?"

"I could use him, yeah, but I was wondering if anybody wanted to join in and see, ... you know, maybe test this guy out and confirm if he's one of yours or whether I can hire him over at my end. I always feel guilty keeping the psychic ones."

"You haven't managed to keep any of those for very long yet, have you? I never thought we would have that many available, but they seem to be coming out of the woodwork."

"I don't know about that, but definitely a few are around. Maybe they feel a safety net is in place for them or something."

"I wondered that too," Terk muttered. "Anyway, what did you need for the job?"

Levi sighed. "Remember Kim?"

"Sure, and?"

"Her brother was traveling through Finland, and he's gone missing."

"Okay, and why do we think that's suspicious? He's a young single guy, right? Maybe he's just wandered off on his own for a while."

"He is all those things," Levi confirmed, "and you already figured that out. Wait, hang on a second, Terk." Levi took a moment for a side conversation. "What do you mean?" he asked someone on his end, and that was followed by some mumbling and bits and pieces of conversation that Terk couldn't quite catch.

Frowning as he listened, Terk followed a lifeline that came up against a blank wall. "*Huh.*"

"What *huh*?" Levi asked.

Ice popped into the phone conversation. "I'm here too, Terk. Is he alive?"

"That's …" Terk stared at the blank wall. "He was, but I'm getting a blank wall right now. I'm not sure what that means."

At that, Cara looked over at him and explained, "If a lifeline hits a blank wall, it usually means a major injury, and he's in between life and death, but I'm not getting that same sense."

Terk extended a hand, and Cara and her sister, Clary, both grabbed on, their energies zapping through his system. He closed his eyes, feeling their combined energies working through this lifeline.

"We have a signature on him," Terk shared, "but something definitely is off at the other end."

"Yeah, and that's what this guy who contacted me was getting at."

"Explain."

"His name is Walker, and he told me that I needed to go deal with something in Finland. At the time, I didn't know anything about it. I felt as if he was almost pushing me in a way. He wants to work for me on this job, but I didn't have a job there. But then Kim came forward and said her brother was in Finland. So I wondered if it was related somehow, and that's when it came back that Kim hadn't been able to contact her brother at all."

Terk asked, "Levi, when you say Walker, did you mean Walker Habernack?"

"Yeah, do you know him?"

"Oh, I know him all right. He's got some pretty good precog abilities."

"But then why wouldn't he have known ahead of time?"

"He's likely contacting you because he's seen something down the road. What does Kim have for information?"

"Her brother went over to meet some special healer in Finland, and that's when he went missing."

Terk looked around the table, as they all stared at each other. Terk's gaze landed on Calum, who immediately nodded.

"I got this one."

"Levi, Calum will meet Walker in Finland. We'll need the details on Kim's brother and anything else you've got as soon as possible."

"You got it," Levi said, "and, Terk, Kim's family—"

"I know. That's not an issue. We'll pick up after this and see. Stay in touch. Calum will be on the way soon." After ending the call, he looked over at Calum. "You're sure?"

Calum nodded. "Absolutely. I'm in. When it comes to family, you know we're always there."

There was no arguing with that.

This concludes Book 4 of Terk's Guardians: Langdon.
Read about Walker: Terk's Guardians, Book 5

Terk's Guardians: Walker (Book #5)

Having precog abilities didn't guarantee having answers, but it did mean Walker knew when trouble was in a specific area. In this case it was Finland and involved someone associated with Levi and a friend to Walker. So he wants in on this job – even if Levi doesn't have a job there. Yet. However, a quick phone call to Terk confirms Walker's suspicions. And he's already on the move.

Ashley's life should have eased up with her move to Finland, but that same wariness creeping back in her life made her feel hunted once again. A strong healer, she helped those who showed up on her doorstep, telling them that she believed the healing energy brought them to her.

However, she'd long ago learned that not everyone who showed up at her house wanted the best for her. So, when Walker shows up, she's not sure what to believe, but it's quickly all too clear that her life is in danger.

Should she trust Walker? No, but she has to make a choice, and the wrong one could kill her …

Find Book 5 here!

To find out more visit Dale Mayer's website.

https://geni.us/DMSWalker

Author's Note

Thank you for reading Langdon: Terk's Guardians, Book 4! If you enjoyed the book, please take a moment and leave a short review.

Dear reader,

I love to hear from readers, and you can contact me at my website: www.dalemayer.com or at my Facebook author page. To be informed of new releases and special offers, sign up for my newsletter or follow me on BookBub. And if you are interested in joining Dale Mayer's Reader Group, here is the Facebook sign up page. http://geni.us/DaleMayerFBGroup

Cheers,
Dale Mayer

About the Author

Dale Mayer is a *USA Today* best-selling author, best known for her SEALs military romances, her Psychic Visions series, and her Lovely Lethal Garden cozy series. Her contemporary romances are raw and full of passion and emotion (Broken But … Mending, Hathaway House series). Her thrillers will keep you guessing (Kate Morgan, By Death series), and her romantic comedies will keep you giggling (*It's a Dog's Life*, a stand-alone novella; and the Broken Protocols series, starring Charming Marvin, the cat).

Dale honors the stories that come to her—and some of them are crazy, break all the rules and cross multiple genres!

To go with her fiction, she also writes nonfiction in many different fields, with books available on résumé writing, companion gardening, and the US mortgage system. All her books are available in print and ebook format.

Connect with Dale Mayer Online

Dale's Website – www.dalemayer.com
Twitter – @DaleMayer
Facebook Page – geni.us/DaleMayerFBFanPage
Facebook Group – geni.us/DaleMayerFBGroup
BookBub – geni.us/DaleMayerBookbub
Instagram – geni.us/DaleMayerInstagram
Goodreads – geni.us/DaleMayerGoodreads
Newsletter – geni.us/DaleNews

www.ingramcontent.com/pod-product-compliance
Lightning Source LLC
Chambersburg PA
CBHW070340200726
48294CB00003B/728